Books by Albert Mobilio

Poetry
Bendable Siege
The Geographics
Letters from Mayhem (with Roger Andersson)
Me with Animal Towering
Touch Wood

Fiction
Games and Stunts
The Handbook of Phrenology (with Hilary Lorenz)

GAMES & STUNTS

Albert Mobilio

BSE

ISBN: 978-0-9898103-4-0

BSE Books are distributed by
Small Press Distribution
1341 Seventh Street
Berkeley, CA 94710
orders@spdbooks.org | www.spdbooks.org | 1-800-869-7553

BSE Books can also be purchased at
www.blacksquareeditions.org
www.hyperallergic.com

Contributions to BSE can be made to
Off the Park Press, Inc.
972 Sunset Ridge
Bridgewater, NJ 08807
(Please make checks payable to Off the Park Press, Inc.)

To contact the Press please write:
Black Square Editions
1200 Broadway, Suite 3
New York, NY 10001

An independent subsidiary of Off the Park Press, Inc. Member of CLMP.

Publisher: John Yau
Editors: Ronna Lebo and Boni Joi

Cover image: Mannerist Concerns, 2008. Collage by John Ashbery. $16\frac{3}{8}$ x $16\frac{1}{2}$
inches. Courtesy Tibor de Nagy Gallery, New York, NY.

Design & composition: Shanna Compton, shannacompton.com

Contents

One plays only if and when one wishes to. In this sense, play is a free activity. It is also uncertain activity. Doubt must remain until the end, and hinges upon the denouement.

—Roger Caillois, *Man, Play and Games*

Balloon Bust

Stand with the others in the fenced-in yard. Shoes drag through gravel and dust rises with each slow step. Each of us has an uninflated balloon. At a signal, given from someone outside the fence, from someone who used to be in here with us, we all begin to blow up our balloons. Faces puff with exertion as the limp fingerlings grow into balls and crescents. A few close their eyes; others study the dilating shapes, the red, blue, and yellow forms, newly entering the domain of things. But all share this sense of fresh arrival, an awareness that, as it pushes away from our lips, room must be made in the world for this balloon. It is our breath and effort, a portion of our life force contoured and made colorful.

Yet it isn't ours at all; it's a balloon, a thing among things, not you or me or anything alive. The contestants blow and lungs empty. We pinch the mouth-like opening and snatch another draft of air. We continue until the first balloon bursts, its explosion causing a stutter among the others' determined exhalations. The blower of the first balloon that bursts is the winner and that is acknowledged by a celebratory detonation of our own balloons, most often accomplished by squeezing and tearing the thin rubber. The yard erupts with random pops. We are red-faced, depleted. Outside the fence, another signal is given and we move into single file and begin walking. Dust billows around our feet and covers the pretty shreds of color that have fallen there.

Light Touch

Two players kneel facing each other. Each one holds a lit candle in their right hand. Their faces appear to be animate in the flickering light. Each of the two holds his left foot in his left hand and raises his left leg clear so as to balance himself on his right knee only. At this time, both may regard one another with candid indifference. Through an open window, hammering is heard. Both men are encouraged to embroider upon the sound. Imagine, for instance, the shouts of hardy men. Of singing as a barn is being raised. Clamorous neighbors carrying picnic baskets. Bold red shirts and gingham dresses splashing against the soundstage sky. The orchestra cues seven brides to take the hands of seven brothers as they all dance the dance of the just plain folks. Neither player knows that his fellow almost always summons the same recollection. Their knees begin to ache. While both men are in this difficult pose, each player extinguishes the other player's candle with a kiss of precisely aimed breath.

Penalty Match

This stunt for four players is often used as a penalty. Everyone sits close together on the floor holding a bowl of ice cubes, each player touching the dish with only one hand, preferably the hand he or she uses to shake a fist at the sky when feigning fury at the gods. Each player then grasps his ear with his other hand. Then his nose. They repeat this action, first ear then nose, five times. But now the ice has started to melt and the four endure a slight delirium. Synesthetic impressions are noted: the coldness of the bowl conjures for one player a desert scene, blue-green sagebrush impossibly still; another perceives the scent of blown out matches; and another's face stings as if sunburnt. Of course, all participants act casual and refrain from visiting the bathroom where a mirror might help them regain their composure. Instead, they feed one another wet ice, the coldness in their mouths a kind of anointing.

Sharp Shooter

This game is the same as Guessball, except that it adds an interesting method of selecting the shooter: he or she is chosen by the casting of lots, much as, according to the New Testament, the eleven apostles did when looking for someone to replace Judas. Not to replace Judas the traitor, of course, but rather Judas the once faithful apostle. Sharp Shooter's chosen shooter needn't be faithful but should be sharp, that is, effective and well groomed.

The similarities to Guessball are not limited to that game. Guessball is the same as Free Shot, but in Guessball the thrower may be any player as opposed to Free Shot's more restrictive view of the thrower's pedigree. Free Shot varies from Target Practice in that players must lean forward with hands on thighs but keep knees straight. This posture is also maintained when playing Team Guessball, although the teams stand with their backs to one another as they bend slightly forward. This resembles Target Practice except in that version hands on thighs are palms up rather than palms down. In short, Target Practice is to Free Shot as Guessball is to Sharp Shooter: different but the same.

Guessball can be played without the guessing element and still be called Guessball. This is a matter the referee or the nearest player to the furthest player from the thrower may decide. If such a decision is upheld by common consent, the game may be called

Guessball despite being devoid of guessing. (Players may, if so moved, guess about matters unrelated to the game; such guesses about, say, the shoe size of a fiancée, the annual rainfall in Cusco, Peru, or the particulars of an opposing player's personal hygiene all fall within the bounds of non-Guessball-pertinent guessing.)

Sharp Shooter must be played quietly with an absolute minimum of noise. Players often wear earmuffs. This is done not because earmuffs in any way diminish the game's actual noise but because it enables each player to believe that no noise is being made, and that the No Noise rule is being observed. The sharpshooter in Sharp Shooter is permitted to make one small noise: upon shooting sharply he or she may emit a modest chirping sound such as might be made by a squirrel or chipmunk or a cartoon representation of either. The sound is unlike the sound made in Guessball but very like the sound permitted in Free Shot. In any event, the sound should be understood by all players to be one that evidences an achieved goal. It is only subsequent to this mutual recognition that players who have missed their shot may take a "time out" and assess their inadequacy as a shooter, as well as their failure to present as sufficiently *sharp*.

Threadneedle Race

They run, they jump, they play. They are contestants. They contest. To win is sweet and noble; to lose, less noble, a good deal less sweet. This game is simple but still a test—of speed, dexterity, the ability to concentrate on the task at hand. There's Jack. A winner even when he loses; he loves to play. This is the lie he tells himself. Jess would never lie to herself because she's pleased with everything she does, says, and thinks. She's pleased as punch. Is discretion the better part of valor? Discretion and resentment, according to Frank. He would rather lose and find fault with the winner than to win and have others find fault with him. Sandy's the same but not. That is to say she's inclined to win, to reap glory, but her faint wishes barely animate a patch of fast-twitch muscle. Sandy wants to come out on top but couldn't care less about anyone coming out below. On the other hand, Bean is a winner. Born to beat the world or whatever defeated portion of it he can dance victorious upon. That this dance is gleeful is the lie he tells himself, although he would barely be able to discern this lie from the teetering pick-up-sticks pile of deceptions that passes for his personality.

How the race is run: two players dash twenty yards across the shiny ballroom floor each to a table on which a spool of thread and a needle have been placed. This distance is short but they must be prepared to brake and redirect their effort toward a less strenuous, more delicate task. Energetic legwork gives way to a different power, one that steadies hands: they must snap off a length of thread, thread the needle, and replace it on the table before running back to the starting line. Jack gets to the table first and bloodies himself with the needle. Fussing over the mess—blood quite undoes Jack's equilibrium—allows Bean just enough time to accomplish the job. Bean's fine with a needle in far worse carnage—hiking in the Sierras, he had occasion to stitch a small gash on his calf. When Sandy and Frank go head to head, both prove deft with needle and thread. Someone in Sandy's college dorm noticed her mending a button and nearly every guy in the building brought her something that year. Frank covered a jacket he wore in high school with a dozen skateboard patches—and then pulled every one out three weeks and a broken arm later. Skills are coupled to flaws. One player impresses at the starting line, another shines in the final heat. They will run, jump, and even sew. They will play at playing well past when playing isn't playing anymore.

Grab a Pin

One is a chaser; all others are runners. Bean is a chaser. You bet. All the time—straight out of bed, big strides, big breathing. He swallows yards of daylight and slips through the dark like a pickpocket's hand in some mark's pocket. No red light is red enough to keep him on a curb; he moves into, no, he moves *at* traffic. "Come on," he says to the laggards who wait for the hard-charging bus to pass or stop. "You've got to judge it right. No one wants to hit you. Come on." The chaser is within a circle, and standing within the circle are ten or more Indian clubs, placed at random. This is where Bean needs to be: confined with the possibility of escape. Enclosure excites him—within a cramped kitchen, an elevator, an embrace, he tenses against the nearness of the world, its warm buzzing skin. It's a kick but only in as much as it promises better. So he's out of there, off in pursuit of sweeter, stronger heat.

Bean may be crazy. Or at least a kind of crazy. The kind that makes you want to be wherever you're not. That's what Jess thinks. And maybe, she thinks, she's crazy, too. Because she also suffers the nearness, how everything surrounds you. Out under a broad swipe of night sky the dark bears down. Her skies are always falling. The apprehension doesn't excite her, though. Instead, she has to fight being tired. At home she'll pull the covers up over her head and try to push through to thinner air, into a place with elbow room where maybe stars aren't right around you and you need to squint to see better because they're so damn far away. It doesn't work. There's too much of her and too much of everything else. After a few squirmy minutes she has to get up and move around. Run water in the sink, raise and lower the shades. She opens a kitchen drawer and puts tablespoons with tablespoons, tea with tea. She rolls her thumb in the hollow of the one that doesn't match the others.

Jess would like to be a runner if that means squeezing out from the always in-between. That's where she finds herself with Bean—sort of with him, sort of not. She quietly dotes on the long *shesh* in the word *dash*, drawing it out over a long exhalation. The sound has *sheer* in it, *shine* and *shoot*, too. Buoyant, gravity-less words.

They will try to steal the clubs without being tagged by the chaser. If they succeed, Bean remains caught inside the circle. The same circle he's been in since the game started ten minutes ago yet it has felt like an hour. With an Indian club in sight Jess aims for it, crouching, running, the awkward gait cramping her legs as she dangles one arm low enough to graze the tips of the grass. The blades are wet and the club is slippery. The neck would be best to grab, but instead she has hold of the wide base, or almost does. A bent, ungainly thing, she further complicates the locomotion by looking up and there is Bean. Teeth bared like headlights, he shifts into her path, his panting displaying more effort than he would like to show. As they close in on one another, he reaches out, the anticipated tag already palpable; Jess shrinks back, her torso twisting away from him. Down to her molecules, she wills herself smaller. The two of them could be dancing, or falling. Or they could be about to get as near to something as you can without quite touching.

Bull-in-the-Ring

The bull is inside a circle formed by the other players, who hold hands firmly. And this bull charges at the linked arms until breaking through and achieving—from a Calvinistic point of view—only a delusional sense of self-determination. But for the purposes of this day, this scruffy patch of unkempt lawn, the delusion is enough. Jess clamored to be the bull; she believes she knows the bull's motivations and can best manifest that purposefulness. She bears down, produces a kind of snorting noise, and affects an impression of great concentration. Or so she believes. For Jess this means an unblinking stare, rather than the more typical squint and furrowed brow. Concentration, she has determined, appears gently anticipatory, an openness to whatever's next. That her wide eyes and otherwise lax features suggest catatonia more than concentration remains unknown to her. At work—she's an assistant to a food stylist—she makes food look pretty for magazines. But pretty isn't the same as delicious: she paints grill lines on steaks with paint stripper, hides white spots on strawberries with lipstick, sprays pancakes with Scotch Guard so the syrup drips just right. There's only one way to get a turkey to look crispy brown, Jess will tell you, and that is with a blowtorch. *I'm good at that*, she says.

Upon breaking free from the enclosure the bull must flee and the others must pursue. (So much for self-determination.) The player who catches him becomes the next bull and the old bull joins the newly composed circle. The bull must break *through* the hands, and is not allowed to go *over* or *under* them. More than cheating, that would be undignified. You may ask what happens if the bull is unable to break from the ring. Players of games like this usually possess the spirit of giving a fellow a chance. This isn't contest rigging or mere empathy; there's gain to be had for everyone. If the bull can't escape, then no one else can be the bull. It's good to escape, even if the act is mere simulacrum. If the players were sticklers, or fanatics, they might keep their friend encircled for hours. They might frustrate and enrage the bull. The bull might then be given to weeping or calling out for the holy mother of God. The circle may become an arena in which a friend exhibits gross abjection thus souring everyone's amusement.

So if Jess has difficulty they will naturally ease up a bit. No one wants her to slam repeatedly into the human chain; to see her fall back and stumble, to rise again, grass-stained elbows, her eyes wide as nickels, moistened by exertion and anger, and again crash into her increasingly resolute friends. No one wants to see this. Or mostly no one. A spirit of camaraderie and enlightened self-interest should be inculcated by the leader. This round, that's Bean. But right before Jess's third attempt he shouts "Hold tight! No slack!" And the gang holds tight and the bull, at least for now, must return to the center and ponder again who is the weakest among them.

Hunt the Slipper

All players but Jack sit in a circle close together, with feet drawn up and knees raised so as to form a tunnel underneath the circle of bent knees. They pass a slipper from one to the other through the tunnel, trying to keep it hidden. Something about this ready-made tunnel strikes Sandy as unnerving—how easily a pocket of hiddenness can be made in plain sight. She laughs because everyone does yet stiffens in response to the newly made coolness below her bare legs, registering its kinship to caves, basements, and things unspoken.

The slipper isn't glass or golden. Not one used for ballet or tightrope walking. An ordinary slipper. Torn seams, sole soiled from trips across the sidewalk to toss trash or the times it's traveled all the way to the Bagel Delight on the corner. This slipper smells slightly of baby powder. Jack stands outside the circle and tries to follow the slipper's covert passage and tag the player who has it. He doesn't give a damn about the slipper or how he'll be able to trade places with whoever he tags. What's happening in his head is what he cares about: there seems to be a hockey puck sliding around the ice rink beneath the dome of his skull. Every movement—he bends down or charges forward—sends the disc caroming into the wall, the reverberation pulsing around his eyes. He can still taste the sweetish rum they were passing around, but not in his mouth—the taste rises up from his stomach. *Where is that damn thing?* The lights have been turned very low and he can't even make out where people's legs meet the floor let alone anything else. Better to follow the movements of shoulders than try to follow the slipper itself.

The bunched up thing comes Sandy's way, the thin flannel cuff immediately familiar because the slipper is hers. She would have preferred not to use it—she might as well pass her socks around, too—but it's her apartment and who else would have a slipper. Did Jess flinch the tiniest bit when it was in her hands? Sandy could swear she saw that. Could swear she saw a flicker of distaste. Jack darts this way and that, incorrectly tagging where he's sure he discerned the telltale dip in Jess's shoulder, then Frank's friend, and that friend's friend. He really needs to sit and let his headache have its way but just as he's about to give up, he notices Sandy's downcast eyes. She's unaware, caught up in some faraway thought. He tags her, or really, because he has to lunge, he slaps her on the shoulder.

"You've got it," he says. Without looking up, she offers the slipper. There's the scent of baby powder. The inside worn smooth. He starts to put his hand inside as if it were a glove but he doesn't. He shouldn't. He knows that.

"Didn't mean to hit you," he says.

"That's okay." Sandy takes the slipper back. "Let's hide something else."

Here I Buy, Here I Bake

This game is Bull-in-the-Ring with a dramatic element added. Because who doesn't crave drama—the old *Sturm und Drang*, conflict and peril. This will be blood-sport and winners will emerge red-mouthed and heaving; the fallen will be cast low, their shame as painful as their wounds. So what be this fresh twist? The bull touches a pair of hands, saying, "Here I buy." He moves to a second pair of hands, touches them, saying, "Here I bake," then a third pair with the words, "Here I make my wedding cake." Suddenly he lunges at a fourth pair, crying out, "Here I break through."

Here I break through. A strong, declarative statement; place and purpose enunciated with efficient syntax. Putting the *here* at the sentence's beginning, with its hard *h* sound, articulates the goal as fixed and definite and, most importantly, preexisting the first-person pronoun which is merely subordinate to that goal. *Break.* A decisive word. Moderate but undeniably clear. *Smash* or *crash* suggest unnecessary mayhem. But *break*, carrying as it does the potential of *ache*, is sufficiently threatening. And *through*, an airy syllable, almost an exhalation, signals what's to be gained— unfettered movement outside the circle's dire constraint.

That's the stuff of drama, the primitive cry of human contestation echoing across centuries. Less of a primal echo down the ages is *Here I buy*. Again, the structural inversion puts the player's destination at the forefront, but the act itself is less, well, less ancient and bloody seeming. Buy what? you may ask. Is this Westhampton lawn fronting a house recently (unjustifiably) profiled in *Architectural Digest* a good spot to be buying anything? The only potential merchants are other picnickers who have brought very little that might serve as merchandise. One might buy a pair of flip-flops or those rather smart-looking sunglasses worn by the guy with the daub of zinc on his nose—an unfortunate concession to cancer fears that ruins the otherwise intimidating effect of those smoky gray lenses. You could buy those or maybe some of that tasty potato salad the stuck-up couple that arrived in a Prius is hoarding. Spooned barely a bite onto your plastic plate! Perhaps barter might be done: Say you know the admissions director at a much sought-after preschool; say you know her very well. The couple with the potato salad has a toddler—presently gamboling in the grass despite repeated frisking by mom for ticks—of eligible age. The mother is an editor at a prominent publisher where your recently penned history of the gondola has a snowball's chance in hell. A mutual scratching of backs might be arranged. Here I buy, indeed!

But what of this baking? *Here I bake*? The context is more uncertain. There will be no baking done on this gently sloping patch of earth where the nearest electrical outlet is in the guest house at least forty yards away and a fire warning is currently in effect for the county. The food preparation in this instance must be understood as metaphorical. To bake is to generate heat, to change the molecular behavior of potential foodstuffs so as to render them more fit for consumption. To bake then is to transform, to—dare we say—transubstantiate. We have moved from the material realm of exchanging goods and services to the more elevated plane where essences are remade; thus, we are in the ballpark—or in this case on the lawn—of the sacred.

Consider the middle-aged gallery owner who excuses his careless efforts to contain the bull by claiming that he's off-balance without his orthopedic inserts; the tawny co-ed, daughter of the pediatrician and therapist, whose pissy manner proclaims the effects of her over-determined childhood; the therapist herself, whose trustworthy visage belies her ferocity in the ring; the journalist with his endless chatter about currency markets and their role in the coming apocalypse; and all the others, too. We stand in this open place, our faces bared to the sun, and receive a kind of Eucharist in this notional baking. *Hoc est corpus.* Joined to this thought are the excellent mozzarella paninis brought by the woman garbed in what she called a skort, a skirt that is really a pair of shorts! A clever gal, she listened patiently to our well-argued case for putting dog runs on a pay-for-use basis.

Another sacrament is inscribed in the penultimate challenge: *Here I make my wedding cake.* Imagine these words uttered at volume by a stubby arbitrageur with a glistening forehead and fire-plug legs. His bellowing returns our attention to matters procreative. And this is both right and good. If the beast is to break free of the ring, if the players who constitute the ring are to hold fast and resist him, if the battle is to be epic and brim with dark consequence, then there must be a pause when players draw strength and moral sustenance from the prospect (at least for the victors) of state-sanctioned (or at least cake-sanctioned) copulation. Within that lubricious, pneumatic, and redemptive act lies the original drama, the battle of body versus soul.

The exquisitely battered fried chicken, the newly divorced blog editor who reminds us that a tank top needn't be relegated to the 1970s, the hope of a ride home in a more spacious, air-conditioned vehicle rather than the sauna-on-wheels we arrived in, the property owner's frisky hound that left paw prints on a brand new pair of linen pants—such things bid our hidden emotions to come forth. So we struggle and dine as combatants of legend once did, or at least until the bugs get really bad or our ride is returning to the city.

What Tree?

What tree is found after a fire?

Ash.

What tree is nearest the sea?

Beech.

What tree is sweet to the taste but aesthetically revolting?

Treacle.

What tree grows near an amusement park?

The one that wasn't cut down to make way for the Tilt-A-Whirl.

What tree is a carpenter's tool?

Plane.

What tree does everyone really like, including the gang at the Dairy Queen and the guy there who sells mushrooms and weed?

Poplar.

What tree is often found in bottles?

Cork.

What tree is the one from which bird droppings soil the village smithy?

The spreading chestnut.

What tree is less than the sum of its many parts?

The conjectural tree that made the One True Cross that was splintered into so many relics over which men have fought and died that it probably holds the record, tree-wise, for the most mayhem caused by a tall, woody plant.

What tree can be found on a tree farm?

A lazy, cowardly tree, one disinclined to brave the unpredictability of the forest where trees don't rely on nursemaids to water and mulch them but rather withstand drought, lightning, wind, and weekend hunters shooting blindly when they hear a twig snap or, in bygone days, the depredations of teenagers with penknives hoping to immortalize their after-school make out sessions by gouging paired initials in a living thing older than their grandparents.

What tree is a body of water?

Bay.

What tree is stupid?

The tree whose branch whips back into your face when the jackass you're hiking with lets go of it.

What tree hides the child who is annoying his father by refusing to leave the park so he can go home and turn the kid over to mom while he opens a beer, secures some cold cuts, and settles in to watch a vintage car show relieved that the outing is done despite knowing that the boy and his mother will soon join him on the couch and junior, still grimy from the sandbox, will paw at the imported prosciutto as the TV guy describes a 1930s Bugatti Atalante, how only seventeen were ever made, and mom will ask about the mother who was supposed to meet him and the boy at the park and he won't want to confess he avoided her and her monster spawn and did so by lurking behind the very tree his son did later?

A sometimes useful but other times less so tree.

What tree sprouts full-blown from your sister's forehead with metallic leaves that change into fiery tongues whose groaning sound could maybe be that same sister repeating ever more urgently, "Are you okay, are you okay?"

The tree conjured by the mushrooms you bought at the Dairy Queen.

What flower is a bird and a riding accessory?

Wrong game!

What tree, what big-ass tree, felled by gale-force winds, falls directly in front of you after you've disregarded televised warnings (not to mention those emphatically delivered by your spouse) about going out in a storm because the media always exaggerate and a little wind and rain aren't going to keep you from buying the lemon sprinkle cake you crave?

The tree of knowledge.

What tree marks the advance of time?

Date.

What tree when it flowers calls to mind the wisdom of our ancestors?

Mulberry? No, maybe not. Was going to say rosewood but mulberry came up. Let's go with rosewood. Then again, first thought best thought, so let's stick with mulberry. Wisdom, ancestors: mulberry. Rosewood, too. And . . . witch-hazel. That's the first thought after deciding on mulberry and rosewood, so it's another first thought. Final answer: pignut hickory.

What tree sighs and languishes?

Pine.

What tree is a couple?

Pear.

What tree is an insect?

Locust. Or how about, "What tree is a plague?" Remember *The Ten Commandments* with Yul Brynner and Charlton Heston? Locusts, frogs—those seem bearable. But the river of blood would be a bother.

What tree is older than most others?

Elder.

What tree is the straightest tree?

Plum.

What tree puts us in mind of life's arc of birth, aging, and death, as well as our smallness when set within the Great Chain of Being?

The generic tree cited in poems written by authors unhappy with the state of their career, love life, and bank account.

What tree grieves most?

Weeping willow.

Chair Creeping

Frank sits on a straight chair facing its back and wraps his legs about its rear legs. He bends slowly backward until his head almost grazes the floor to pick up a handkerchief—pinched up like a pyramid—with his teeth. In this vulnerable and physically distressed state he manages a wish for an amount of money that would allow him to live the life he believes he should be living. Once an upright position is regained he removes the handkerchief from his mouth and drapes it over his eyes as he speaks aloud the monetary figure while picturing that life: the custom shirts he should be wearing, the masseuse he should be employing. No more throwaway umbrellas; no more roll-your-owns. Profligacy with paper towels. His new life summed up in the barely sipped scotch left with a crumpled twenty on the bar. Frank plucks the handkerchief as if he were lifting away an old face so a fresher visage might appear in its place. A face that won't show his curiosity about what others have that he lacks.

Elimination

Two equal teams take the field, although just what is meant by equal remains ever out of conclusive reach. Each group forms a circle or a square, except that one individual from each team—in this case it's Jess and her colleague Doone, both armed with fly swatters—takes up her place within the area of her surrounding opponents. Evoking the melancholy of missed chances and forgotten infatuations, a muted trumpet blows to signal each of these two players to begin to chase and swat opponents. Doone wears a sailor's hat and clip-on sunglasses; her shirt is tied above her bare belly. Very *Where the Boys Are*. Jealous of her style, her talent, and her success, Jess introduces her to everyone with undisguised pride. Some of the hunted will seek deliverance from danger by declaiming their belief in the essential harmony of all life; others will spit and kick wildly at their pursuers. And there will be those who take sides against themselves, their dividedness rendering them paralyzed on the field, unable to cry out or flee. They look about at others like themselves, immobilized, but there's no kinship, only the piercing sense of their own debilitation, as well as the smell of fresh dirt raised by so many shoes tearing at the grass. As soon as a player is swatted he leaves the game. Among those on the sidelines, humiliation gives way to enigmatic longing. Undeterred, the swatters continue until one of them eliminates an entire team and thus scores a point for her squad. Honor is rendered; winners enjoy water ices and shiny ribbons. Teams form again and the process is repeated until everyone has had a chance with the swatter.

Cocked Hat and Feather

The players locate and patronize a standard bowling alley such as might be found at the local strip mall. Cocked Hat and Feather is played with four pins: three are set up at the corners and the fourth, a duckpin, in the center spot. The leader approaches the manager of the alley—he is likely a middle-age man rotund or thin, friendly or preoccupied, with a ski-slope nose or one that isn't so readily described. He might be a she and if so, the same applies with an additional possibility that she may be wearing a macaroni bracelet that her niece made last month at summer camp and she's only wearing tonight because she had to stop by her sister's house before her shift and she's always looking for ways to prove she's not jealous that her sister has children while she doesn't.

The leader says something like this to the manager: "We're out on the town tonight celebrating our friend's divorce from her deadbeat husband who hasn't worked in three years but still finds the time to play in fantasy leagues for every major sport. She's a big-time fan of Cocked Hat and Feather and we could play a few rounds if you allow us to reset the pins and to employ these duckpins we've brought along; they're smaller than regulation pins and made of wood. They harken back to a time when simple people made simple things and the subject of social class wasn't fit for polite conversation. Your accommodation would return some long-departed mirth to our friend's marriage-weary life and would cheer us up, too. And, oh, very nice nose and/or bracelet."

The standard pins must be placed at the three corners and the duckpin in the center and please be sure they are thirty-six inches apart. Most likely no one brought a tape measure so the most lithe among the players, the one with the ardent yet oh-so-distant look in his eyes, is pressed into service. He is asked to form a mental picture of a football field and then tighten the zoom down to one-one hundredth of that field. To then imagine that turf directly in front of him, to spread his hands wide, then bring them together until they tap the edges of that image. That's thirty-six inches give or take an eighth. He will hold his hands still, kneeling down at the end of the alley while another player uses him like a yardstick.

The object of the game: The bowler tries to knock down the center pin and scores nothing in any frame in which she fails to do this. Given all due preparation the actual game often strikes participants as insufficiently complex; if so, perhaps adding elements of improvisatory dance or Latin conjugation would elevate the challenge. Certainly, it was no easy thing to find duckpins, or, more to the point, to endure the puzzled looks given in junk and antique shops after inquiring about *duckpins*. But players, who have donned sporty windbreakers and clipped their ear hairs, may desire more than a contest offering fellowship, fluorescent lighting, and the comfort of molded shell seating. It may not be enough that the figurative hat is cocked and that it sports an equally figurative feather. There should be vertigo. There should be a climax. An opportunity for purity.

Pat and Rub

This is an old-time stunt. An easy, arguably childish stunt. Yet it offers in its simplicity delight in our biomechanical essence. Okay, it's a pretty dumb stunt. It directs the stunter (the hunter hunts, the punter punts, so . . . ?) to pat the top of his head with one hand and simultaneously rub his chest or abdomen with the other. Complexity may be introduced by instead rubbing the head and patting the belly, or by reversing hands. But Jack is no tap-dancing Olympian gymnast. Doing this stunt—that is doing it right, keeping a fully circular motion on the belly and a ruler-straight pat on the scalp—demands focus and he's not one to underestimate its requirements. He has been trying to pat and rub himself for years with mixed success.

To pat is to do one thing and to rub is to do something else that's similar but different. You pat and rub when you do them both at the same time. For instance, you strive to kiss your supervisor's ass to get ahead all the while you're firing off résumés from your office computer; or you sleep with any and everyone you can all the while chastely dating your marriage-worthy co-religionists. Pat and rub. The feat involves a certain cognitive dissonance, perhaps a dash of duplicity; you have to work each angle with a steady hand. Jack tries. His current, ongoing example: He wants the people he knows, loves, to like him and to love him back. But he also wants to finish a book he's been writing, a book about these people that will show he knows them well and loves them less than they would believe. He's been writing it for two years and the day it's published is the day his friends—the people he turns to every day—will never speak to him again.

At home Jack writes a sentence about someone very much like Jess: "People she sees on the street or on the train, she tells him, look sad and awful, their veiny noses and rolled down socks, she could almost cry, not because she cares but because she's relieved she doesn't have to know them." He reads those words and recalls when Jess said that to him. He would like to change a detail, tilt it this way or that to be less recognizable. But maybe he doesn't know how or doesn't have the imagination. He types, reads, and deletes it as he thinks of Jess, of her eyes—slightly hurtful, slightly hurt, mostly uncomprehending of either feeling—when she said that and how he wanted her more then. Then he types it again. Deletes it again. Pathos versus anti-pathos. Wanting versus hating that want. How do you make one hand do one thing and the other do something else? The stunt is an old one; children do it best. Mostly because they don't care how dumb they look. But Jack does. And there's the rub.

Story of Crows and Cranes

A field. Clouds shaped like clipper ships. Two teams. They stand three feet apart, one team on each side of a neutral zone about three feet in width. About ten yards behind each team a goal line. The ships make stately passage across the autumn sky. Red and gold leaves litter the grass and if anyone paused to take in the surrounding trees, the lowering sun, they would be overwhelmed by a heavy sense of melancholy. No one does, though. Although Frank, hands in pockets, stares away from the game and watches a pair of hawks swoop in ever-tightening circles. One team is dubbed the crows, the other the cranes. The alliteration pleases the ear and players on each team—in a fashion sociologists have long probed—immediately begin to think of themselves as, say, the crows—a group of varyingly acquainted folks who now share a group identity and commitment. *When you're a crow, you're a crow all the way.* The leader, presumably a partisan of neither species, but really, at some fundamental level doesn't she have an affinity for either the jet black bird, its putative intelligence, and prominence in folk tales and songs, or instead the balletic water fowl, with its improbable comportment and dexterous maneuvering in the hunt? It is difficult to imagine someone indifferent to the question of the birds, let alone the actual persons populating each team. Impartiality is almost always a fiction. Especially so, in this case, when the leader, a woman who has been recruited by Jess, is a photographer whose livelihood, like Jess's, depends on the ability to make heaps of joint compound look like grandma's mashed potatoes.

The leader tells a story and from time to time she will use a word beginning with the sound *crrr* . . . and then complete the word. If it is *crows*, then the crow team flees across the zone through the defending cranes toward the goal while trying to avoid being tagged. Vice versa if the word is *cranes*. The tale-teller should linger on the syllable, draw it out for maximum anticipation. For instance, a sentence might go something like, "And there along the old wooden fence were several squawking crrr . . . ." Bodies on both teams tense, ears perk as the *r* vibrates in the cool air. But this isn't the signal: "Were several squawking crrr . . . azy men just escaped from the nearby prison." This ploy might draw a player into a false start, charging into the neutral zone; that eager beaver is considered tagged and should—if the rules are followed to the letter—be subjected to great mocking. Their looks, lineage, and any personal details involving sexual fetishes are all fair game. Caution is advised; Jack takes note.

The leader—she was introduced as Doone, but Frank heard it as Doom and is wondering what kind of parent does that—stands arms akimbo, looking quite the arbiter, at the head of the neutral zone. Doone begins to spin her yarn: "The child was an ordinary child as children go. He wore hand-me-downs that fit too tight so he seemed to burst from his clothes. This made him look awkward and for this he was teased by other children in the way that children do. One morning on the way to school he traveled down a narrow lane between two houses as he always did. In one building lived an old woman who grew peaches in her backyard, ate them on her porch, and spit out the pits with great ceremony; in the other lived a pretty girl who didn't go to school but looked down from a dormer window on the top floor and the boy could hear piano music coming from her house."

There is a good deal of fidgeting among the players. Some rub their hands and cup their ears; others crouch and stretch; all note a drop in the air temperature yet she continues: "On this ordinary day as days go, the boy decided to stop and visit the girl. As he approached her house the music was clearer and he thought it as pretty as the girl in the window. He waved to her and she waved back. But he heard another sound, too. A sound that was not pretty—a noisy, wet eruption." Doone's face evidences due disgust.

"Are you fucking kidding?" Bean says not quite under his breath. He's cold. No socks; guinea tee, as he calls his shirt.

"Shut up," Jess says.

The wind can be heard making its way through the woods at the edge of the field—you can hear it a good while before the closest treetops sway. The leader rejoins the tale: "The boy, as boys will do when confronted with things impolite, begins to laugh. A tiny laugh but the old woman hears it and she laughs, too. The jollity of each fuels the other." Frank shakes his head. *Did she say jollity?*

"The boy's hand-me-down shirt grows smaller around his chest. Soon their mirth drowns out the sound of the piano music. He looks up to the dormer window but now it is closed. 'Oh no,' the boy cries out. Just then the girl, as pretty as pretty girls are, pushes open the door to stand on the porch. Her hair is long and black and seems alive in the soft rays of the early morning sun; she looks down at the boy and across the lane to her neighbor and shrieks, 'I am sick of your shit you dirty old crrr . . . .'" The consonants call the players to attention. They lean forward as if to snag the rest of the word from the air. "'Crone!'" Doone pronounces loudly and repeats, "'You dirty, filthy old crone.'"

Puppet strings dropped, the players go limp. Except for a guy nobody knows, a friend of somebody's friend. He bursts across the zone with triumphant cheer only to pull up short, look around expectantly, and await the derision. But impatience has made everyone itchy. They just want some goddamn action. Besides no one knows anything about him, except that the way he's standing there wide-eyed, grinning, he's too ready to be abused. There's no heart for it and more to the point, no material. Doone doesn't drop the thread: "The old woman's face clenches, taking on the woody texture of a peach pit. Out of the folds of her apron she retrieves a kitchen knife, a long one as kitchen knives go. The boy jumps to the porch and throws his arms around the pretty girl's waist, his ill-fitted shirt tearing across the back. And there, exposed and flagrantly black is the tattooed image of a crrr . . . ow!" Doone leaps up as if to propel the word toward the echoing sky. The crows tear into the cranes' defenses, now laggard given the long delay, and everyone makes it to the goal.

In the midst of desultory celebration Jack takes Jess by the arm. "Who is this person?"

"She's a really cool person. I work with her and I liked that story," Jess says. "It was . . . ." She is still searching for the word when Frank sidles up. "Who names their kid Doom. I mean, isn't that child abuse?"

"It's Doone. What's wrong with you?"

"You mean like Lorna?" Franks says. Bean breaks into their circle. "I'm cold as a witch's tit," he says. "Anyone want any?" He holds out a pint of whiskey.

"Hey, look." Frank lifts Bean's outstretched arm. On the bottle a solitary, contemplative bird adorns the label that identifies the brand: Old Crow.

Spin-the-Plate

Players are numbered consecutively. And their heavenly father knows the number of hairs on their heads. One stands in the center of a circle formed by the others. This individual has a plate that she spins atop a short pole while calling a number. The person whose number it is (who probably began their Sunday with hopes of finishing overdue yard work, getting the car waxed, then maybe an afternoon nap) tries to catch the plate before it falls to the floor; if he succeeds, he gets to spin the plate. Spinning a plate is not without its challenges; most people can barely get it going for a few seconds, so this game is often limited to those gifted with a robust sense of balance and commensurate dexterity. Jugglers, fly fishers, phlebotomists, money changers, meatball sandwich makers, and flagpole-sitting banjo *artistes*—these are the types with the requisite skills. Bicycle messengers, icepick testers, and wind chime assemblers have been known to do in a pinch, but these groups usually insist on an outdoor venue. If a suitable open-air venue isn't available, they have been known to ask the audience to blow ever so softly. Needless to say, it can be hard to gather a sufficient number of souls to play.

To spin is an art, but to catch is a duty. Consider the situation of the person whose number is called: he or she must try to catch the plate before it lands on the floor. So there you are, confronted with an ill consequence—but hardly a catastrophe since the dish is decorated with Huckleberry Hound and Boo Boo Bear and is not grandma's commemorative wedding plate, the only item salvaged from the house fire that killed her pet toucan. Do you want to be called? Probably not. You want to remain on the sidelines, out of the fray, you're no hero. Okay, maybe if you found yourself on a subway platform witnessing someone threatening someone else. What was that bright glint in that guy's hand? You shift from foot to foot, crease and re-crease the ticket stub in your coat pocket. Your number is being called. Will you step in at the ready? Or is that one plate you're not going to save from its crash?

Matching Halves

You do not wish to be alone, but instead long for contact, communication, some modest diminishment of your sense of estrangement. At a VFW hall, high school gymnasium, or in this open lot behind a big box store you seek your match. Upon arrival, there are others, not grim-faced, but open, receptive. A man and woman, sporty, youngish, step forward. With his watch cap set as symmetrical as a halo, he resembles the draw-the-lumberman, except for his heavily tattooed neck; her unzipped windbreaker bears the name of a local medical facility, the free clinic you sometimes pass on the way to the car wash. She smokes with intention and her hard draw conveys a wary regard. "Okay, over here," she says, as her partner beckons with one hand, the other occupied with what seems to be a garment problem in his pants' front.

The assembly numbers about twenty, all unfamiliar faces. One has the sense that these are neighbors more likely to be out-of-doors in the evening than during the day. There is one recognizable face—a teenager often seen outside the local pharmacy where he appears to transact some kind of business. Tonight he's as fidgety as he has been in the past; head bent, he carries on an animated conversation with the asphalt.

The hosts call everyone together and distribute pictures cut from what appears to be magazines and old books. Each picture has been cut again so attendants are in possession of half of a whole image. You are then instructed to find your partner for the evening by finding the person who holds your other half. You have the top portion of a color illustration from what must be an anatomical or surgical manual; it shows an open abdomen, the flesh pulled back by hook-like instruments to reveal ropy intestines, a dun-colored liver, and a kidney bean-shaped stomach. The remainder of the body below the intestines is in the hands of your soon-to-be familiar. In earnest, you begin the search.

The first inquiry is directed at an angular woman whose thick blue eye shadow may have been applied in haste. "Excuse me," you say, leaning forward to catch a glimpse of the page she holds. "Are we a match?" She is underdressed for the weather. On this crisp early autumn evening she lacks a jacket and only wears a muscle-style shirt. Her shoes are complex looking, with a good number of shiny buckles.

"You want a match?" And before you can clarify, she hands you her picture and produces a lighter and some sort of translucent pipe. "Here you go," she says, putting the flame to its bowl. Her picture is decidedly not a match as it presents a partial view of a gleaming bathtub and is likely an advertisement for a cleaning product. She places it to your lips and again summons the flame.

"Suck. Suck hard," she says.

The inhalation burns hot or is it cold? Like swallowing light, light that's strong but flickering. And that spreads to your chest and head. Your new friend retrieves the device and forms a practiced embouchure around the stem while you shift from foot to foot; your picture, you discover, opening a clenched hand, has been squeezed into a ball. Another young, similarly garbed woman wearing several earrings arrives. You both reach through the exhaled smoke.

"Hey!" she says. "It's coming around. Here, hold this." Into your hand she places a torn page and there it is—the lower half of the figure. The image is intimate though the gender is indeterminate. Where there might be anatomical precision there is instead vagueness—an elliptical yet undefined mound. You unfold and smooth your picture and align it with hers. They are a match. Every eye in this little group widens to mark the moment. Halves have been made whole. The pipe comes your way again while you reflect with escalating pleasure that the forecast for an evening chill has been proven quite wrong.

Broom Lever

Feet together, hands at his side, Jack stands as if summoned to this spot. In one hand he holds the handle of a broom, its business end resting on the floor. He volunteered to go first because he's handy with brooms. Growing up, sweeping was his household chore—to broom out the kitchen, his father's workroom, the back porch, the driveway. He did so meticulously and with fervor, taking delight in moving debris and dust into small piles and then working those accumulations into greater sums, all the while maintaining a military front as he crossed the floor, advancing from the flanks, bringing up the center. He knows a good broom, a tight brush made of crisp straw bristles (not plastic) with the slightest give where the sweeper meets the handle.

With his arm straight, he must lift the brush end of the broom gradually from the floor until the broom and his arm are at shoulder height. This stunt gives a strong man a chance to demonstrate his ability. Jack is a strong man. A strong-*ish* man at least. A strong-*ish* man who keeps a clean, well-swept apartment, maintains his fingernails at the cuticle, and who will, when he has the opportunity, steal underwear from the drawers of women he knows, wear them a few times, and then find a way to return the items to a laundry basket in their homes. He has this routine down cold, in fact. Starting when he lived in a group house in college and over the years, Jack honed his surreptitious technique. The secrecy itself became a precious possession, a talisman that conferred the ability to understand other secret keepers. Whenever a revelation appeared either in the news or among his acquaintances of a shameful or illicit act, he felt kinship.

There have been times when the theft was exciting and times when the wearing offered the more piercing thrill. Standing in a near-stranger's bedroom easing a hamper or dresser drawer open in half-light or going out on a date aware every minute of the thin elastic's tenuous encirclement—how could he say which supplied the more galvanic kick. But surely the topper had to be getting caught by and confessing to Jess.

The difficulty can be decreased, of course, by using a lighter broom or one with a shorter handle. That's not Jack's style with brooms; he is, after all, sort of strong. The night Jess caught him in her bathroom, sitting on the edge of the tub, his arm plunged deep into a basket of clothes, he would have crawled down the drain if he could have. Or at least at first. So vibrant was the sense of shame—its heat flooded his face and chest—he felt emboldened by its voltage. He stood up and held out a clutch of nylon and strappy things and said, "Do you think you could help me find something nice?" Never before had he been this calm with Jess or any woman. Their friends could be heard down the hall and the bathroom pipes groaned—the upstairs neighbor must have flushed—and a guttural sound rose through the tile walls and crested abruptly. It was just the answer Jess had been searching for and she began to laugh. A nervous, what-the-fuck-is-this laugh, but Jack knew one thing—that Jess would listen if he wanted to explain. He wasn't sure right then if he wanted to, but he would be in time.

Small cheats are permitted: for instance, the broom can be lifted more easily if grasped at a certain distance below the end of the handle. Jack doesn't take this opportunity. Instead, he begins to lift at the very end of the broom. It is difficult. There's no doubt about that. He envisions himself as a construction crane, his bones and muscles are gears and steel cable. Eyes closed, he keeps the image vivid. The strain radiates from his wrist into his shoulder and upper back. But when, as Jack has done, you become a machine, you don't worry about nursing a torn tendon in your forearm and offering a feeble lie about how you incurred this injury. That's not how a strong or strong-*ish* man thinks.

The broom and Jack's arm quiver as they rise; as the broom approaches waist height the movement quickens. He has to resist his biomechanical imperative—the urge to crouch. If he lowered into a squat, he could thrust upward with chest and legs pitching in. Another unacceptable cheat. Jack is shaking all over as the straw—he can see flecks of grit in the gray balls of dust bunched in its base—reaches his eyes. All he has to do is straighten his arm—to hold out the broom in one level line from shoulder to the tip of the broom. A few inches more . . . Jack is sure he can do this. He sucks in and holds a fistful of air and his face tenses as he is revealed for what he is: a man who knows what to do with a broom.

Make Him Take It

Two rivals—think Cain and Abel; Holmes and Moriarty; Homer and Ned—start with a row of fifteen matches. If the danger of igniting a house fire looms too large (after all, people are *playing with matches*), sewing needles may be employed. Worst outcome: a few drops of blood on the carpet. Then again, you could use fifteen matches that have been struck and doused. This might be safely accomplished in your home's least flammable locale—the bathroom. Done, for an extra measure of caution, in the bath-tub. To guarantee against all mishap, fill the tub with an inch of water. Prospective players remove shoes and socks and, while they're at it, potentially flammable items such as shirts, skirts, and pants. They can then—without fear of incident—stand face to face (each keeps watch on the other to ensure a stray spark doesn't kindle boxer shorts or bra) and strike the requisite number of matches. Of course, in this close proximity, there is the danger that a lit match may come in contact with exposed flesh. The actual injury that might follow would be slight—a minute patch of singed skin. But the likelihood that a player's shock at being burned causes an arm to jerk or leg to kick, an action that destabilizes the pair, is great. It's well known that most home accidents occur in the bathtub and the discovery of two semi-nude adults, bones broken, bloodily entangled on the bathroom floor, lit and unlit matches strewn about the bodies, would only add to this grim statistic. Best to use the nonflammables such as sewing needles, razor blades, or if they are available, toothpicks.

The players take turns in removing, let's just call them *items*, and on any turn may remove one, or two, or three. Each tries to force the other to take the very last item. Like taking the last lamb chop from the serving plate at a family dinner, taking the last of whatever's being used for this game brings similar opprobrium. But there is a difference—the lamb chop is desirable; to take the last one is to deprive others. To take the last *item* is to pick up the leavings. The former, the shame of gluttony; the latter the shame of doing another's bidding. Being compelled is always less than desirable; being compelled to do something utterly arbitrary and meaningless—pick up the last *item*—brings the coercion to the forefront. The exchange between the players is about nothing more than I *rule you*.

Since the duel is as much a puzzle as a game (the player with first pick has and can employ a mathematical advantage that precludes the player who goes second from ever winning), the victory is an intellectual triumph. This further burdens the loser with shame; it is one thing to be strong-armed; another to be strong-armed by your opponent's computational skill. Or at least that's what you think, as you are unaware that you were enticed to play by an insecure, covert browbeater who knows that first choice, once attained, will permit him to engineer a series of defeats that will leave you self-doubting. Do you really understand compound interest? Are you known to waiters all over town as an under tipper? Is your daughter letting you win at chess? Questions about your computational abilities assault you in the wake of your fifth loss. Recollections of high school report cards swim into focus. You are a dunce, a sad specimen. You have been made to take it.

But then again, if you are playing with needles or toothpicks, you have successfully avoided dying naked on a bathroom floor. And that is no mean accomplishment.

Ball and Bottle Relay

Jack has never been quite so ill at ease. His team has six empty, small-necked bottles, three of them with a golf ball resting on top. Jess and Bean are members of the opposing team, one similarly equipped. They stand close to one another, talk purposefully, sharing recipes for healthy but easily prepared meals. No more empanadas from the food truck scarfed down while waiting on line for Belgian waffles; with the quick tips they're exchanging they will soon be brown-bagging homemade low-cal nibbles. The two of them already glow with the salutary effects of the wholesome foods they're talking about: blood sugar concentrations settle in at recommended levels; fat-to-muscle ratios grow ever more optimum.

Jess transfers the golf balls one at a time to the second group of bottles and then tags Bean, who moves them back to the original bottles, and so on until everyone has shifted all the balls. With some surprise, not ever having handled a golf ball, Jess notes aloud its rough texture and studies the dimpled surface. She rolls it across the tips of her fingers—it's rough *and* smooth. She thinks of skin, its many imperfections, the way it serves as a record of daily life: a palm scalded by a hot pan handle; a calf bruised exiting the shower. Noting the look of altered things—that's her métier. "Beat that," she announces, the last ball in place.

Jack knows golf. His father watched hours of golf on TV; didn't play, but loved to watch. Said he liked the grass and trees and pretty little lakes. So Jack knows that the hundreds of indentations on the ball cause micro-eddies of air upon being struck by the club. This turbulence allows the ball to rise—that's what lifts a plane's wings—and sends it down the fairway further than the ball would travel if it were smooth. He might try to explain this to Jess, but he doesn't wish to intrude between her and Bean. A brief disquisition on aerodynamics may not be the best way to remind her of their past affections.

In this case, Jack concludes that turbulence hinders rather than encourages his ability to go further. Unlike Bean, who slides past a brooding Jack. No less nimble for his speed, Bean holds his ball like some kind of rare specimen between thumb and index finger and places it neatly atop a bottle. Jack arrives behind him and angrily slaps at the row of bottles and sends them flying. "Smooth," Bean says, stepping clear of the mess. "Like a baby's ass."

Circle-Pursuit-Race

Some kind of circular or other closed running course is needed; a course can be improvised by marking it with lawn chairs, ornamental deer, gnomes, discarded tires, or other obstacles. The runners are stationed at equal distances around the course, each with his own starting line. There is, owing perhaps to the general absence of a sound eschatological vision on the part of the players, no finish line. Frank aims himself, legs pumping, toward something he cannot see, but that fact in no way diminishes his determination. Failure has long hounded him, worked its way into the smallest corners of his life. He'll drop a dish, cut himself zipping his jacket, climax too soon, sign his name where he should have printed it—barely noticeable misses and mistakes, yet quite noticeable to him. He keeps track, he knows the cumulative score. Idling in line for coffee or in the shower, he closes his eyes to see a long list of check marks in black ink scrolling by. *Demerits* they were called in high school. Merit minus. Always less than.

The whistle blows and all begin running at once, and each runner tries to overtake and tag the runner in front of him, while also avoiding being tagged from behind. Frank finds himself, then, amidst. Catching up yet almost caught. Pivoting to his left at one of the deer, to his right to skip past a lawn chair, its aluminum frame fluorescent in the sunlight, his breath comes in bursts. Frank lunges at Jess who has stumbled just in front of him. Of course, he stumbles too, tripping over her legs, his outstretched arm skidding into the turf. Just behind him another runner brushes his shoulder. "Tagged!"

The game continues, round and round the course, until only one player remains. One of the deer looks directly at Frank, or at least that's how Frank sees it. He bears down and squarely meets the reproving gaze of the durable polyresin replica. Buoyant voices chatter away around him. Jess is saying something to Bean about a book she started reading but couldn't finish because there were too many semi-colons. The sun exhales and in doing so swells larger on his brow alone.

Pom-Pom-Pullaway

A piece of earth on which two parallel lines are marked about sixty feet apart, with sidelines about fifty feet apart. Apartness. The sensation marks Jess's sense of herself in the world. She's popular, sure. And she knows that. People she hasn't seen in years invite her to weddings and add handwritten notes to say how much it would mean if she came. At her old job folks *loved* Jess; even the mailroom guy who seethed at everyone when he rolled his cart past their cubes sometimes stopped at hers to cough a bit and apologize with words almost indistinguishable from the coughing.

Sandy takes her position in the middle of the field and issues the chaser's required challenge, "Pom-pom-pullaway, come away or I'll pull you away." The singsong quality she hears in her voice is cause for sudden but unnecessary embarrassment; how else utter so alliterative a threat. Put those words in *Scarface* and Pacino would have to croon them just the same. No matter, she is acutely aware that Jess heard the trilling notes. The sun eases through scattered clouds mottling the meadow's slopes and Jess stands slackly, hand on hip, in a blanket-size patch of shade. A casual indifference seems to dictate every angle and curve; she looks like she was poured into place. If Sandy could see Jess's face she's sure she would find no more than a hint of a smirk because for that girl a smirk is emoting like Sarah Bernhardt. Sandy doesn't want this in her head about Jess but it is. *Look at her, just poured there.*

Once her call is complete, the runners make a beeline for the goal behind Sandy while she tries to tag someone three times. If she does that person joins her for the next call. Jess is close enough to pursue—in fact, she's the closest player—but does Sandy really want to do that? But if she doesn't her disinclination will be obvious. The decision, though, is made by Jess who comes on hard, buoyed above the high grass by long, loping strides, right at her friend. The clouds have freed the sun's full force and the entire field vibrates with sudden warmth and thrumming feet. Sandy runs, too, aiming to meet Jess at an angle, but she can't keep that line of attack because Jess matches her, side-step for side-step, to keep them on track for a head-on collision. She's playing chicken, Sandy realizes. *She wants to see me duck.*

Despite the elegance of Zeno's paradox—one always has half the distance to their goal to travel therefore they will never reach it—these two players will surely meet. Zeno will not intervene to reassure them that when they are, say, the width of a molecule apart, they still have to traverse half a molecule and a quarter molecule after that and so on. He will not alight twixt them to guarantee no bruises today. Sandy extends both arms; either way Jess moves she wants to be ready to reach her. Doing so slows Sandy's stride but that doesn't matter—she only has to tag the woman now bearing down on her, shedding her last traces of insouciance. The air is heavy, yet Sandy detects a quickening swirl beneath her flung-apart arms. Is that what pilots call *lift*? Jess is half of a half of a half away and Sandy believes that if she were to leap she could be airborne.

Hotball

A variety of balls is used. Jack appreciates this—there is too little variety in his life. He wakes, works, wanks, and sometimes thinks about just how much money he would need to never have to think about money again. Same, same, and then more of that, he says, and he knows that in repeating this complaint he compounds the problem. He knows himself too well, yet self-knowledge has proven a poor recompense for the effort. He knows which toenails grow faster than their neighbors; he knows the dream he dreams in which his penis is washed down the bathtub drain and understands that its import is merely metaphorical yet still he showers carefully; he knows the names of the assholes who hung him by the arms from a clothesline pole in sixth grade and called him Blowjob Jesus because he answered Sister Roberta's question by saying the babe was wrapped in *swallowing* clothes; he believes the Germans deserve more character development in American World War Two movies; he knows why she left him, why she came back, and why she's the worse for having done so; that he drinks to make himself sad when he's supposed to be sad, but mostly he's relieved to feel just the way he does when things go bad: sleepy. He is quite aware that he chews loudly; that he plagiarized a college term paper on corporeality in John Donne's "Devotions"; that women find him funny for, maybe, a couple of weeks, and then they most decidedly don't; that he can't keep straight the difference between Van Johnson and Van Heflin, and he fears somehow this speaks to some core intellectual failing; that he hasn't eaten anything with mayonnaise since he read about a busboy who jerked off in the restaurant's supply; and he knows he will not remain an atheist in whatever foxhole he ends up in.

Jack knows his own odor, which few of us really do, but after a car accident and severe concussion he lost all sense of smell for nearly half a year and when he regained it he reveled in himself, his body and clothes, and came to understand the morbid, vinegary scent of water spilled from a flower vase as his own. Jack knows the batting order of the 1964 Phillies; he knows every new day contains spillage from the last; and when all is said and done, when his book of life is written, mourners will say he was well behaved as they look down and notice their shoes are in need of a polish. A variety of balls is used. At least eight and preferably sixteen or more in number. Balls you can change, Jack would say. But you can't change what you know. And Jack knows that when a person holding a ball is hit by another ball he is out of the game. He is kaput. Benched. Done for. And if that person is Jack, he's fine with that. He's fine with sitting it out.

Step-by-Step

Frank knows what love is like. Frank knows it's like a hurricane, like a battlefield, like a rockin' pneumonia. Frank knows love about as well as he knows lyrics about it. He sings along. At the bottom of the basement stairs the players sit side by side. The Odd Player stands in front of and facing the others and catches. There will always be some distance, Frank observes, in matters large and small. In matters Frank. But change isn't outside his ken; there are songs about changing, too. He has been devising lately a plan of self-improvement, one in which he will plow under bad habits (Doritos, day trading, the website Tokyo Topless) and cultivate good ones (wear pants at home, wear bicycle helmet when biking, apply sunblock to forehead, nose, and back of neck). His friends appear restless. He tosses the ball to the person at the head of the queue who will throw it back; if the Odd Player misses a throw he is replaced by the thrower.

No one wants to be replaced, to be set aside while someone else occupies what was once their spot. Being replaced as Odd Player isn't a tragedy; on the other hand being replaced as king, Shakespeare-wise, is the very stuff of that genre. But being replaced in any way (from your corner office, on your street corner, the homey corner of an ex-lover's memories) invariably stings: not only are you revealed as inadequate, but the job is handed over to another person. Whether it's a sister, brother, boon companion, or treacherous enemy—the pang isn't much different; you didn't do what you were supposed to do, so listen up: the bald guy with the earring, the retired woman from the florist shop, the spacey kid with the Ivy League degree, the sleepy-eyed girl that used to wait on you at the coffee shop, Bob from Baltimore or is it Philadelphia? Well, they're *replacing* you. Your place—however fine, however shitty—is their place now. *Adios, pal.*

Of course, Frank is aware of this impending problem only at the subconscious level, the level just below his attention to the throwing skills of each player. Will they return the ball with an ineffectual lob or a smoking-ass pitch? And the incoming balls themselves, often aimed (Bean is such an asshole) right at his face. Little League traumas—*Christ, not that kid at first base!* a parent long ago moaned as Frank took his position at the bag— are never far from any test of hand-eye togetherness. Too much has always hung on how quickly he can sight and snatch a ball.

The basement smells fetid like a kitchen sponge after very dirty dishes. Coming down the stairs he had walked behind Jess and pressed forward to inhale her outdoorsy scented shampoo. He drew deeply until the rec room's sticky brew overpowered the simulacrum of an alpine dell. Behind him Bean asked, "Close enough?"

"What?"

"Why don't you take a bite?" Bean's tone is often that of a

command, but one double-dipped in irony. The easy kind. Like a boot camp sergeant doing stand-up for high school kids.

The warm flush began to invade Frank's face. He knows what others see—cheeks and ears as if freshly slapped. It's a betrayal, really. Your body shouldn't serve you up on a platter.

"Bite me," he said. Of all possible comebacks this one's failure was as evident as his shame-stung mug. Worse yet, Jess turned at the bottom of the stairs and looked him square. *Oh, shit.*

"Not you, I meant . . . not you." He stammered as that awful time between them, her attempt to coax his reluctant cock and the errant incisor that made him yelp, spooled out in a mental instant along with his certainty that she, too, pushed the same replay button. No evidence she had, but she never shows much about what's happening inside.

"Hey, people of earth, move." Bean glided past them, eyes forward as if he couldn't care less about anything not right in front of him. Jess pinched Frank's collar and said "Hey," a gesture that seemed both rehearsed and genuine. That awkwardness was maybe all his; he never could tell. He just never could tell.

There is no penalty for a thrower who misses. Only the Odd Player must worry as the ball crosses the length of the rec room, sometimes in a lazy arc, other times thrown hard, straight and mad for winning. The penalty is for lack of coordination, for lack of anticipation, and for lack of reasonable expectation. For these deficits in basements and in bedrooms, you are replaced. No matter. Frank is primed to field incoming. Bits of songs ping around in his head—*ball of confusion, great balls of fire, the morning sun comes risin' up like a red rubber ball*—and he takes a long chewy breath that tastes like something old. Whether the balls come fast or friendly, Frank can rest assured: there's always a place for him at the back of the line.

I Doubt It

Some lies are more entertaining than others but they are still untruths. Some puppies are cuter than others but they all still bark. The gradations of difference among lies, dogs, and pretty much every perceivable thing in the universe constitutes the nature of human judgment. This stray perception—prompted by an overheard and neatly botched proverb ("Let sleeping logs lie")—occupies the dealer who begins by taking from her hand one, two, three, or four cards, *supposedly* of the same rank, and placing them face down on the table, announcing their number and supposed rank, saying for example, "Three Queens." She is not required to tell the truth and the other players must decide if she is or isn't.

The dealer's voice and manner should be calibrated with care so as not to divulge veracity or lack thereof. In this effort one quickly anthologizes memories of cop shows and movies in which lie detector tests are given. Certain obvious cautions are immediately evident: avoid sweating, shifty eyes, fidgeting, and crying out "Alright, alright, I did it. I killed him." Instead, relax, make eye contact with the inquisitor, smile but not in a self-satisfied, I-killed-her-and-can-lie-about-it-as-calmly-as-ordering-eggs-over-easy way. The smile, indeed the overall facial presentation, should aim for that casual deployment of features just shy of bemusement. Just shy, though. Full out bemused not only screams guilt but does so with a taunting cherry on top. Dirty Harry or Popeye Doyle is going to smack the twinkle out of your eyes if you get all bemused.

When any player wishes, they may call, "I doubt it." This is preferable for reasons of sportsmanship to "You filthy purveyor of prevarication," yet this locution surely expresses a more honest reaction to a suspected ploy. After all, this is not an entertaining lie, like for instance, the cheating husband's confession to his wife following her discovery of a woman's gym sock (not hers) in the back of their Subaru when he explains (working up real tears) that he stole his coworker's footwear because late in life he's developed this strange compulsion and is open to therapy to address the unspoken needs that cause such depraved behavior, all of which is infinitely preferable (but not without its own cost) to the truth: he and Sally in sales were knocking boots in the parking lot and afterwards she must have grabbed a sock from her bag instead of a tissue and left it behind. Caught red-handed, out of desperation he produces a lie marked by style and verve; it is a lie worth listening to. Especially choice is the exculpatory and not-a-little accusatory detail about his wife's fondness for lingerie being the start of his fetish's slippery slope. However, the smart money is on the failure of this well-turned deception—the wife isn't buying it because the Nike anklet in question gives off the distinct aroma of a fuck.

At this point the cards in question are turned face up. If the doubter is caught lying, the player takes the cards back; if not, the doubter adds to their own. Truth be told, a few cards are but a modest reward for ferreting out a liar. We do good for good's sake, of course, but thinking sociologically in terms of large-scale institutions versus the modest power of individuals, well, there's a real need for a more concrete incentive. The self-satisfaction and social esteem in which the doubter basks might be burnished with, say, the provision of a Herman Miller Aeron desk chair. If that seems too extravagant, perhaps a cheese-of-the-month club membership, an all-in-one remote control, or, if the player's finances fall short of his aspirations, one of the better made cellphone cases.

In any case, attention must be paid, otherwise the doers of good deeds, the citizen cops around the card table, will find less and less reason to finger miscreants and expose their misrepresentations. On the other hand, the successful card-dealing liar is also due more than a paltry gain of cards. In as much as we should encourage the skeptical eye in search of justice, the artful spinning of bullshit shouldn't go unremunerated either. It too is a bedrock element in our lives, one worthy of nurture. Deception beguiles and turns us from daily chores, from the prospect of mortality, and might prove a saving grace when an errant sock requires an explanation. That husband's lie, one whose elegance and gratuitous complexity stands in inverse proportion to the garment's lowly utility, represents the kind of craft acquired only through lifelong practice. You apprentice at card tables in youth and work your way up to job interviews and marriage vows. "Two hearts and a club," says the dealer. Always keep in mind: all calls will be made in rapid succession, without hesitation, except when play is interrupted by a doubter. And when that happens, lie harder. That's when the game quickens the liar's pulse. Almost as much as it does for the player being lied to.

Storming-the-Fort

The fort is a line of gymnasium horses, parallel bars, curio cabinets, beat up lawn mowers, and other similar obstacles. The obstacles should not be too high, nor should they be too low, nor should they be just right, as such a notion appeals to a normative objectivity unrecognized as viable by players and game masters alike. Where necessary, the obstacles should be shrouded in black crepe, as befitting those objects (e.g., a tire, an ottoman, a treadmill, a corpse) that remind us that life itself is an act of mourning the relentless increase of the inanimate around us. Players form two teams, one in a line about twenty feet from the obstacles, the other just behind the assemblage. At a signal, the attacking team rushes forward and tries to climb. They must go over, not around. The defenders try to prevent the assault from succeeding. To do this they may go anywhere they choose. Maybe home, to a hot toddy and an uncracked copy of *Middlemarch* that will be read, it will, it *will*.

In any case, all manner of holding or blocking is permitted, anything, in fact, except hitting or other forms of aggressive roughness. Unexpected intimacies—kisses blown across the gym horses, suggestive winks while in a clinch with an opposition player, or frottage, but only light frottage, such as might be acceptable at a freshman high school mixer—are also permitted.

The defending team tries to prevent the attackers from getting over the obstacles. They may climb, push, or repurpose personal grooming items as weapons (only to be brandished in as much as one can brandish, say, tweezers). This is the way of the world: all against all, winning isn't everything, it's the *only* thing. But the struggle is not so grim. If the attackers do not triumph in a pre-determined period of time—oh, about two minutes of appropriately Darwinian mayhem—then the two teams reverse positions. The shame of defeat flares but briefly in the players' inmost selves; they will surely strive again and some Homer—could it be that ginger-haired lass who smells faintly of doused church candles—may perhaps someday sing of their brawny exploits.

Bean Bottle Throw

The number of stars may be infinite; the number of beans to be used is fixed. There will be ten. They are dried and hard but their color and relation to symmetry can vary. They are lima, they are pinto; they are kidney; they are coffee and chili. They are any one of several dozen kinds of beans that might be easily acquired and deployed in this test of skill. There is nothing particular about any one choice, only that the bean exhibit a beanly essence; a beanness, so to speak. This farinaceous seed is to be pressed into non-edible service, as beans often are in bean bags, bean bag chairs, or as bingo beans, counting beans, or metaphorically, bean counters, bean balls, or the beans one might be full of or spill depending on metabolic or moral inclination. A literal bean counter provides each contestant with ten and, after confirming the number, assessing the shape and aerodynamic character of the bean, she turns her attention to an upright milk bottle placed four to five feet away.

The bean will be aimed and launched with the intention of entering the mouth of the bottle and thereby scoring a single point. Much whooping may attend the successful accomplishment of this task. The excitement is likely to build if a contestant continues to—over that distance of four to five feet—pitch beans into the container. It is possible though, that a player or two or three will attempt to distract the bean thrower, to disturb their concentration and calculation as they prepare their toss. The devilry flaunted by poor sports is a sad testament to the growing lack of respect for bean-based competitions. A few of the more typical tactics include: standing close to the bean thrower and shouting loudly about the decades-old government conspiracy to make Americans increasingly docile by the manipulation of daylight savings time; standing close after having doused oneself in lighter fluid and holding a lit match; kneeling behind the bottle begging the Lord of Hosts to visit locusts upon the home of the thrower; and stripping bare, painting the extremities blue, and gyrating to Joe Turner's song "Flip, Flop and Fly" directly in the thrower's line of sight.

While distracting, these methods are not the worst witnessed. There is a report of one competitor asking another if she has ever brought owls to Athens; another details an individual who quietly wept in his car in the parking lot outside the game emporium and thereby disconcerted arriving players; and even more shocking is an instance when a contestant advanced an anti-Copernican argument with the fervor of a Jehovah's Witness who is under quota for converts and being threatened with transfer to a neighborhood where "Armed Response" signs are visible on many lawns. The thrower in that case sent all ten of their beans so wide of the mark that several passersby came under the impression that a burrito had burst in the vicinity. The bounds of propriety and fair play were irretrievably crossed and all the competitors in that match were inconsolable for days afterward. They spoke of anger-soaked dreams in which anthropomorphic planets took turns reciting Moody Blues lyrics.

Such behavior was not what Bean Bottle Throw, Bean Drop, Bean Shooting, Beanbag Three-Two-One, Quincunx Bean, or any of the multifarious family of bean-to-target endeavors was ever meant to incite. Rather, the sport was designed to reward skill and engender pleasure. These antics pervert that goal, diminish its players and fans, and ultimately denigrate the blameless bean itself. Observe the bean when thrown; its rotational progress toward its goal should inspire us. The bean may be small, may be merely a seed, but the bean moves through space with a purposeful yet insouciant grace. Know the bean, know its longing for the bottle, for a place within.

Wall Head-Pivot

A line is marked on the floor about two feet from the wall. The setting is spare, with shadows as solid as a wall and the wall as dark as a doorway through which you might fall. The player leans forward, places his head against the wall, and folds his arms behind his back. The player is Bean and he sets his pate against the wall with some carelessness about its rough texture. Thus arched, arms appearing bound as if he were in a straitjacket, his figure suggests more than a stunt in the making—he looks like a madman bent in supplication. He leans forward determined, the floor and his legs and feet occupying his entire view: the elemental forces—gravity rooting us to the ground and energy propelling us upright. In addition, there is a pair of much scuffed Oxfords worn laceless without socks like loafers. The shoes evoke Bean's past—beer blasts on the quad, summers in Maine, hasty departures from partners just fallen asleep. The lack of laces speaks to expediency; these shoes are kept on by sheer speed of movement.

To perform the stunt Bean must use his head as a pivot to rotate 360 degrees, without moving his head from the wall or unfolding his arms. This action requires balance, flexibility, and some indifference to pain—all qualities he possesses. But before putting them into play he must choose whether to turn left or right. Not a lefty, Bean knows that turning that way will allow him to employ his strong right side for the outset of the pivot, but coming around, when his back is arched against the wall, he will have to resort to the weaker. It is the midpoint of the pivot that most taxes the back and legs; that is when the need for the most tensile strength shifts from right to left or vice versa. The question then is should he begin with strength to establish balance and momentum or might reserves of these prove more crucial when he is self-pinioned and literally bent over backwards. Unlike, say, the ability to tolerate pain, decision-making isn't eased by mere exercise of will. For instance, in high school Bean ran in the 1500 meters with a sprained ankle, all the while imagining his leg was a tuning fork being struck with each downward stride to make a higher and higher pitched sound. Focusing on that thought, on controlling the pitch so that it rose in precise increments, enabled him to race. He finished second.

He turns right. Past experience tells him that some spur at the midpoint of anything—running track, getting through college, copulation—is more important than a good start. The middle is where losers lose. Initially, it's his head that bears the brunt of the motion; his scalp just above his forehead burns and general pressure—consequent upon the weight of much of his upper body—provides felt insight into the shape and construction of his skull. A vague image recalled from an anatomy text reveals the brainpan as formed from several parts rather than one solid battering ram of a bone. This gives him pause but he proceeds.

Not being able to steady himself because the restriction of his arms isn't only a balance problem, it's one of self-control. As he approaches the 180 degree point, getting there by moving his heels in tinier and tinier arcs, his posture becomes precarious: the urge to throw out both arms to save himself from dropping like the proverbial sack of potatoes comes in escalating spikes.

By the time Bean is facing away from the wall, staring up at the ceiling, he is used to the pain around his head. As he pivots the contact point moves too; his occipital—a word that is also emerging from the fog of a long-ago class—is presently engaged. Instead of the supplicant, he now cuts the figure of a celebrant, a dancer in an ancient ritual of sky worship arched in relish and awe of the heavens, his arms set to clap together in ecstatic embrace. But the ceiling, streaked with paint roller lines that only someone set this intently in its direction would ever see, is not the sky. Growing dizzy, Bean closes his eyes, more to keep his balance than to escape the claustrophobic view. He shifts: this is the crossover to his strong leg, more able shoulder. His knee flexes to accommodate the change and he's around the corner. *Fucking A.*

The rest is gravy. Turning back into the wall enlists gravity, and the natural inclination to lean forward rather than back. When he's back where he started—beneath him the floor, his shoes— he notices the need to breathe; he'd hardly been breathing and for the first time he notices the boiler's oily smell. There's no one to cheer or laugh with about this. Bean is alone in the basement of his apartment building. The narrow, sidewalk-level windows have grown darker. He reaches for the string below a nearby bulb. Maybe, he thinks, one more time. Now that he knows the trick of it.

How Do You Like Your Neighbors?

The circle. Sitting in one. The player at the center bears the unfortunate moniker *odd man* or *odd woman*. Those in the circle are neighbors. How long have they sat? It goes on for days. Not quite, but that's how long some might say it does. All players might contemplate why we spend our days, if not our entire lives, being places we'd rather not be, doing things we'd just as well not. Sandy certainly does. She realizes the question presupposes that we know where or what we desire. Maybe the gnawing sense of being detained and deterred doesn't require a "from what," just a "not this." So we chafe at having to sit still not because we actually want to walk around but because we don't want to sit. Thusly does she brood, teeth dug against her lower lip betraying her tussle with paradox.

Such questions hardly plague Bean. Not that he isn't aware of these knotty matters; he simply finds himself gifted with the ability to leave them be. Presently, he is the odd man at the center. The descriptor is one he savors for its roundness and depth. *Odd*, he sounds out to himself. A plucked string on an upright bass, stirring the air. The tactile, that's his realm. He takes everyone in with a quick turn and begins the game with the question (one, perhaps, as old as Cain and Abel) "How do like your neighbors?" The question is directed at Jack and he supplies the requisite answer, "Oh, not so well," referring to the players on his right and left—Frank and his sister who is visiting from out of town. Then the odd man asks "Who would you like better?" and Jack names Sandy and her upstairs neighbor. In truth, he has been eager to get closer to this neighbor—she's a real estate agent and his lease is up next month. The rules send them out of their chairs to trade with the undesirable neighbors. So four chairs are up for grabs and the odd man (*ahddd*—it's strumming in your head, isn't it?) tries to snatch one of the seats. If he does, then somebody's left out, and they become the next odd player.

The teasing and laughs, the mischievous pushes and shoves are a shadow play that only hints at the contest's underlying brutality. It is survival of the fittest, the quickest, the most willing to push just a wee bit past the parlor game niceties and make damn sure they get their ass in that chair. Having to sit in the center of the circle—whether or not you like the sound of *odd*—is to be made the object of quiet derision; to be kept there is to be an object of exclusion, too. After one or two rounds (and that's where Bean is now) it's all fun and funny. But by three or four, the player in the center is stoking a low-level anger; and the group he or she was just a member of—the circle gang—has already begun to part ways with their former neighbor. Begun to see a certain justification for the odd player's ostracism: *Why of course*, one or the other thinks, *they really don't know how to play. I mean, look at the way they screwed up this or that in their life.* The room clouds with judgments like this pretty quickly. The odd player registers the thickening funk and the overall aggression accelerates. Earlier, Sandy was at that point in her fifth round and imagining that she would never, ever get out of the center. That she would be there looking sillier and sadder until everyone grew bored and let her go. Hence her fatalistic cogitation over where you want to be. She only got back to being a neighbor by faking an injury—crying out as if Bean had elbowed her chin. Distracted him enough to slide into the chair they were both vying for.

Bean's agitation is growing teeth. He will not endure a sixth round; he will not be the monkey in the middle. The space from where he sits to any one of the chairs is about ten feet. The answerer can make it more difficult by picking new neighbors who are close to them, rather than the far side of the circle. In fact, it is that small grace exercised between friends—when the embarrassment one feels for the odd other reaches an uncomfortable pitch—that usually brings about a change. But no one's lending Bean a hand. When Jack names Sandy and her neighbor they are quick to their feet; Frank and his sister pop up like toast, too. And five people are in motion. You have to be decisive, to pick your chair and make it yours. Bean pushes past the neighbor, pushes past Frank only barely refraining from giving him a full-on body slam. Still, the force is enough to unbalance Frank and tilt him into his sister's determined stride; she knocks him back the way he came and the question of Frank remaining upright is an open one. He might if he can flatten a shoe that's turned out, with his weight on the side of the foot; he won't, though, as

Bean, in passing, drags a leg behind and sends Frank crumbling to the floor.

Around him everyone's found their place. Jack admonishes Bean for the blow but goodnaturedly, in concert with the whole group. There is an undoubtedly squalid aspect to lying on the floor and the hairs stiffening on the back of Frank's neck evidence the feeling. This is the dumb dream where you find yourself naked in public. "Fuck you and fuck this," he announces as he stands. His words cut into the other voices and the back of his neck tingles in the silence. He looks to Sandy—he doesn't mean her when he says this. She's not laughing at all, but she doesn't meet his eyes either. Doesn't want, he can tell, to share in this with him.

"Come on," Jack says. "Don't be like that."

"Be like what?" Frank says. He hears himself, conciliation and defiance packed into that tiny question. "Be like what?" he repeats.

"Be the only one who gets out of this thing." It's Sandy. Wagging her finger, doing schoolmarm, a grin that shades towards grimace. When did she start wearing so much lipstick, Frank wonders out of nowhere. "You're not going anywhere. We're all sitting here until everyone looks like an idiot."

"I'm sorry, man," Bean says. "I'll stay odd man." He starts for the center chair.

"No, no. I'll do my time." Frank takes his place in the middle, the object of sympathetic, well orchestrated gazes. The monkey in the middle. But is there really anywhere else he'd rather be? He just doesn't know. Best, though, to hurry past this awkwardness, take his seat, do his dumb time—then, in what he hopes is a manly, no bullshit tone, he turns to Jess: "How do you like your neighbors?"

Word Endings

After enduring a tedious lecture about the significance of various pen inks (black, Jess maintained, quietly denotes strong opinions; blue, she derided as the lazy choice; and red, the hue employed by folks with serotonin imbalances), Bean, like the others, jots down a list of about twenty word endings. Each is a combination of usually three letters that form the endings of common words, such as *und*, *mes*, *tech*, *nty*, *er*, *wly*, *ose*, *ene*, *ken*, *ady*, *ely*, *ity*, and *don*. He combines and sounds out the syllables to make approximate words: "*Mestechs*," he says, "I've made a few." "It's a *kenunddon* wrapped inside a riddle." "*Adyose*, amigos!" Since the clock is ticking and they must complete their words, one for each ending, no one appreciates his distracting gibberish. A general urging that he stop goes unheeded. "You're no Jack *Kenity*." "*Techund*, to none!" Jack pushes a beer toward Bean. "Suck on this," he says, and a downcast Bean relents.

"The ending of a word is what makes it a word," says Jess. "You're doing something primitive, preliterate until there's an ending. You're breathing heavily so I hear *saah* come out of your mouth. What's that? It's air. But when you add *ound* you're communicating. An infant opens its mouth and out comes *wah*. Nothing. But add *er* and it's saying *water*." She is pleased with this oration and alone among the group nods with approval.

"So a baby isn't communicating until it says *water*?" Jack doesn't quite believe he's responding to her. "The kid is balling and flinging shit at the wall but until it yells out 'Water, goddamn it,' it doesn't know that it wants a bath?"

"That's not what I'm saying. You're making it seem like nonsense."

"Seem?" Jack says. A phone rings out on the street; it's far away but the tune fills the front room where they are sitting. For a second everyone awaits the cessation of the chime followed by a greeting, but the phone just keeps ringing only fainter and fainter.

"But what about *tit*?" Bean inquires, hard on the *t*. "That's a totally comprehensible word and *ty* doesn't add much at all. In fact, it undermines the whole concept with a sense of diminution. Itty-bitty, right?"

The ringing resumes, much clearer now. Again, the expectation. Pens hover over sheets of loose-leaf each with its columns of words, sketches for Towers of Babel. And, again, the ring slips into silence. The pens resume their work, endings find beginnings, and out in the quiet beyond this room someone who wants to speak is calling the person they want to listen.

Concentration

An entire deck of cards is shuffled and dealt face down in rows. The exact pattern, Sandy knows, isn't important. Sandy knows about cards and she knows about quiet. She thinks more about quiet—and why she can't keep it—than she thinks about cards, but she makes sure each card has a definite place. The group settles—Jack and Bean were teasing Frank about his attempt to grow a beard last winter; they've stopped and Frank sits still and inspects his hands with surprise, as if they were newly purchased. And Jess has found a place to pause in a long tale about this guy at work and the guy he hired and why she's pretty sure that the first guy hired the other guy to get in his pants and this first guy always does this but it never works because he hires artsy-looking guys and won't believe Jess when she tells him they're straight. When the talk stops as suddenly as a spigot that's been shut they all notice how the air hums with its absence; Sandy tries to tune into and relax within this gauzy frequency.

She can't. She doesn't trust the quiet and so she says, "I didn't know the boy I asked to the prom was, uh, having sex with my, you know, he was, well he is, my step-brother," but the last few words dissolve in the self-conscious laughter that always devours her awkward attempts to add to any conversation. The ensuing chorus of *whats* and *huhs* lacks much interrogative energy; at this point when responding to Sandy it's merely a reflex because they all know her explanation will only be screwier than what she just said. Frank pays attention, though; he always marvels over how she manages to be impenetrable yet distressingly self-revelatory with the same utterance. He told Jack once, "It's a tonal language—you have to figure out what she means from the stops, starts, and swallowed sounds."

Jess rolls her eyes and lets out a long "Jeez" that skids right up behind but doesn't quite tap the second syllable of "Jesus." She picks two cards and lets everyone see. Two of clubs—so she gets to keep drawing until she selects two from different suits. If you draw, say, a heart and spade they go back on the table in the same place. The player with the most cards wins and that person is the one with the best memory of what cards have been turned over. That's usually Sandy. Most likely this owes to the level of focus she brings to what's right in front of her. She's trying, you see, to keep her mouth shut, as she often does, with whatever meditative method presents itself. Counting buttons on someone's shirt, listening intently for clues to regional accents, studying the second hand on her watch—she tries to keep herself inside that quiet place but invariably she erupts with something oblique and usually disquieting: "You could have sex, you know, just, well, sort of, through the front of those, the pajama bottoms," she told Bean when he was showing her pictures of himself on Christmas morning when he was nine. Yes, the pajamas did have a buttoned-up sailor's flap, but what about Sandy's childhood would provoke such a thought? Once during a discussion of how people can never find their phones at home, she piped up: "I leave my phone in the bathroom because I'm always in there, not for what you think," a gulping chortle overwhelming the kicker, "even when I don't need to be."

Her giddiness softens what otherwise would be off-putting for some. Not Jess, though. That voice—the laugh, the way it smudges whatever silly thing that escapes Sandy's jingle-jangle brain—gets to her, or really gets all *over* her. Sandy's talk is an itchy sweater Jess can't peel off. The confessional intimacy unnerves her. Implicates her; it's as if Sandy was ventriloquizing an inner life Jess didn't know she had. But she's much more bothered by the inadvertency. How does craziness like that slip out? How could your guard be so low? What if Jess just blurted out something like the things Sandy says? Could there be a situation, the right or wrong person, that could cast a spell and loosen words she'd regret? It was frightening. Sandy was frightening.

As the pile of cards grows beneath Sandy's clasped hands, the wrinkles on the back of her fingers absorb her. The deep creases at the knuckles; the other ones like bloodless paper cuts. She hasn't said a word since mentioning her prom and permits herself only a tight anti-smile as she collects another pair. Across the table Jess, too, holds her tongue, holds herself head to toe, and eyes her friend warily. The others—Bean and Jack—are busy elaborating on the kind and degree of Frank's romantic failures.

The two of them hoot and make noise that would suggest a good time. The game continues until all the cards are removed or turned face up, whichever comes first.

Crossed Wires

One instructs; the other obeys. The commands are given in a firm manner that conveys neither a trace of doubt nor a wish for greater power. The tone—as delivered by Jess—is even-tempered, crisp. Bureaucratic. Frank takes hold of his left ear with his right hand and his nose with the left hand. At her bidding, he must quickly release his hands and grasp his right ear with his left hand and his nose with the right hand. The commands come quicker and quicker and the one who obeys grows increasingly confused. And the wires connecting brain to hands do indeed cross. The way Jess fires off the directives, mixing them up—at one point three consecutive commands are all the same—makes a harried mess of Frank's motor skills. He's a crazed altar boy scribbling signs of the cross on himself; he looks like he's afflicted with Saint Vitus Dance. It's a sight. One Jess enjoys much more than she lets on. "Left hand, right ear. Right hand, right ear." Frank cuffs his chin to get this one. "Right hand, nose. Left hand . . . right nose." It's tough for her not to howl along with everyone else as they watch Frank pause, synapses probably throwing off sparks. "Right nose? Bullshit," he says.

If Jess joins in though, then she's part of the fun, part of what's funny to everyone: friends having a good time with only the merest undertones of ridicule, all well within the bounds of acceptable peer aggression. But that's not what she calls fun. The deployment of words rapidly and cleanly enunciated; her sense of control over volume and intensity; her forceful projection of calm—these are the sources of her delight. She's thinking Emma Peel from *The Avengers*: English accent, master fencer, good with a karate chop, dressed in leather head to toe. Ever since she saw the reruns last year when she was holed up with the flu at her sister's house with a cable package, Emma is the shell she wears when she wants to be untouchable. From that steely vantage she regards silly Jack, sad Jack, flustered, self-smacked, mouth-breathing from his efforts. She counts to herself *four*, *three*, *two*, *one* and that's enough rest for him.

"Left hand, left ear. Left hand, left ear. Left hand, left ear," she snaps, almost slipping into ersatz Brit. Repeating the same command throws him back into a mess of physical stutters and starts, his right arm jerking at the ready. "Left hand, left ear." This time she hears how loud she's getting, her own arms are emphatically cocked, as she reins herself in by turning away from everyone and drapes herself in Emma's cool. Jack covers his face with both hands. "I'm done," he says and looks at her looking away. *This is what it is*, he thinks. *This is who I am.*

Sesquipedalia

All players are given the same long word. In turn, each begins a brief pantomime inspired by its first syllable. Frank models himself as if wearing a short dress, running his hands around its bottom edge to simulate the *hem* in *hemisemidemiquaver*. Sandy does jumping jacks to call forth *gymnophoria*. Jess, the last player to take a turn, grows bored and distracted. She's remembering an online video that showed a tidal wave flooding villages along the shore. *Was that Sumatra?* Her spell breaks, the other players consider her vacant demeanor with . . . sympathy? "Malaysia," says Jess, aware now as she hasn't been for a long time of what a poor fit she makes among others. "It was Malaysia," she says. And even as she takes in the puzzled faces around her, she's already occupying a bird's eye view above the shore, the water rushing far below.

Spoon Photography

The mind reader (that's Frank; he believes he's a natural) claims that a person's image can be transferred to a bright silver spoon. A bold claim, to be sure, and one that wouldn't be quite so fantastical if Frank's friends didn't think him the most obtuse of humans when it comes to intuiting anything about anyone, from their desire to be offered a seat on the subway to their wish to be left alone. Playing the part, he insinuates that even he doesn't understand the powers of the reverently held spoon. The picture, he declares, is unclear and only recognizable by, well, your friendly neighborhood mind reader.

If Frank could actually read minds like a book he would not be pleased with the pages in front of him. Opening the otherwise closed volume titled *Jess* would present him with Helvetica—the typeface employed for signage and labeling—because Jess imagines herself to be quite legible and tends to manufacture thoughts in sharp directives: merge left; caution: falling rocks; remove sensation of guilt associated with deliberately provocative flirtations. Planted right in front of her, Frank would read . . . nothing about himself. *I know that spoon*, would be scrolling through her head. *That's my spoon.*

More acutely distressing news would emanate from Bean's noggin: he's looking at Jess, his benignly cast face a suitable mask for the swirl of calves, belly, and thighs that churn behind his eyes with rising and falling intensity. Frank could grow dizzy if he were able to follow Bean's hungry gaze as it raked up from Jess's breasts to her arched neck, open mouth, and closed eyes and down again. But Frank's equilibrium isn't in jeopardy as Frank is no mind reader. (He is a paranoiac, though, which is a kind of telepathy.) Instead of swooning, overburdened by forbidden knowledge, he leaves the room, as the stunt requires. Sandy, his designated assistant, holds the spoon in front of one of the players—in this case Jack—before placing the utensil on the floor. A snicker makes its way from face to face. Frank displays utter seriousness and Sandy behaves hesitantly, resisting her role, as if she isn't an accomplice but a skeptic caught up in a comic ritual that has suddenly become solemn. This actorish affectation, the low lights and late hour, all conspire to create a shared smidgen—just a smidgen's smidgen—of credulity. The expectancy that greets Frank when he returns is almost genuine. He bends to pick up the spoon and studies it intently; there's nothing in its hollow but his own squinty eye peering back. Is this a keyhole to a mystic dimension or is he, in fact, looking past the spoon at Sandy, who according to plan, is supposed to indicate the subject of the picture by imitating that person's pose and actions?

She tries to do just that by crossing her arms and leaning back deep into the sofa just as Jack does. To acquire his sense of ease and self-assurance, she allows her back and legs to slide into what could be warm water; it could be good to be Jack. But she's cautious not to allow her legs too comfortable, too wide a pose. That would give away the trick. She relaxes her hips just enough for Frank to receive the message and when he does he blinks hard and shakes his head as if reeling from the shock of revelation. (Hey, if you're going to play, play like it matters; anyway, Frank is often braced by an over-awareness of others, so for him this is method acting.) As he prepares to impart the name of the person whose image he sees in this otherwise ordinary spoon—one that Jess, still, *still*, is hankering to get a closer look at because she's certain it's hers and that it somehow made its way into Sandy's hand—Frank reaches low to find the right intonation to announce precisely, with excess pauses, "The face . . . that I see . . . is Jack's."

No one is surprised. The spark of expectancy that crackled in the air is extinguished when Sandy unknots her hands and slouches as if she were unplugged. So uncharacteristic is the movement, it diverts Jess's attention from her lost cutlery.

"Sandy, why didn't you just start tugging at your crotch," Bean says.

"You sit like a nun waiting for her spanking most of the time," Jess laughs. "And suddenly you're wide open."

"I mean it's one person out of three," Bean says. "You could have just guessed and gotten it right. That would have been more convincing." He stands, hurriedly fakes a yawn, and shoots toward the door; Jess stands, too, casts an eye at Bean and waits as if she might betray herself with precipitous action.

Frank looks downhearted. He thinks he put on a good show. Thinks the mind reader deserves better for his efforts. He drops down next to Jack. "Sorry, I thought that would be fun." Jack doesn't answer—the wheels in his head are turning as he watches Jess and attempts to gauge the cause of her uncertainty. In truth, he enjoyed hearing his name announced with such drama; enjoyed the jolt of being party to something otherworldly. "It was fun," he says. And then with an importance not unlike Frank's delivery, "Bean . . . Bean is a dick." The two of them watch Jess disappear out the door.

Self-conscious about her posture, her hands, everything about the way she is in the world, Sandy adjusts herself again and again. The three friends sit silently with the realization that nothing out of the ordinary happened or will happen. There is no supernatural. There are only people and the things people do. People come and go, and Jess and Bean just went. Sandy makes her way to her kitchen. She pulls open the silverware drawer and places the spoon in a compartment where it sits awkwardly with unmatched others. Her spoon, the one she exchanged for this one, no doubt fits as badly in Jess's drawer. Tonight, she saw that Jess was curious, that she wanted a closer look. Is she talking about it with Bean right now? Maybe she's saying, "I'm worried about Sandy."

Pure Laugh

All players sit in a circle. One player calls *ha*, then the one at his left calls *haha*, the next one *hahaha* and so on. Everyone maintains a straight face. There is nothing funny about *hahaha*. *Ha* is a sound you might make if you were frightened or surprised or trying to stop an escapee from climbing over the prison wall and it was very cold and you could only get out the first part of *halt* before the icy air seized up your throat. *Ha* isn't funny nor is *hahahahaha* one iota more merry. In fact, if anyone laughs or smiles or fails to produce the proper number of *ha*'s in accordance with the sequence, a point will be scored against them. If you accumulate ten points you must leave the room for an adjacent room. There you conjure memories of recent sexual activities and picture them staged as floats in a parade. Trombones gleam under a high and relentless sun. From the curb you watch your amorous life dramatized by people very much older than yourself. You pay close, very close, attention to the many imperfections of lived-in skin. Through the wall you hear *ha* and know that everyone has just discovered something secret about you.

Hide in Sight

The leader—Frank, the *leader*. The relish he takes in the role is no match for his reflexive ambivalence, as he sets to his task with modest yet pertinent ceremony. He holds aloft the object for inspection, in this case a ring box open to reveal plush velvet and a dark crease where a ring would be. Any small object will do: thimble, a short pencil, coffin nail, nipple clamp, blasting cap, souvenir meteor fragment, apple core, tree ornament, rodent skull, Monopoly piece, calcified tongue of long-dead saint, or snow globe. Anything small but distinct. But not so distinct as to make players envious and ultimately bitter about their own paltry objects. (They would then fall to squabbling and the only things that will end up being hidden are feelings of inadequacy.) Also, it is best to avoid anything in a transformative state, such as a day-old fish head, an ice cube, or a lit match—these are things that either because of their imminent decay, dissipation, or conflagration may not be readily findable. The game should test ordinary powers of detection rather than one's extraordinary ability to pluck out a burnt matchstick from an ongoing house fire. Other more advanced games pursue that aim.

Jess, Sandy, Bean, and Jack study the ring box. Nothing special, they conclude, but Jess wonders where the box came from and where the absent ring is. She recalls an awkward evening (among a few) with Frank when he seemed uncharacteristically testy, given to half-uttered sentences and effortful attempts to make eye contact. "Are you leaving it open or closed?" Bean asks this with measured intensity. Much, it seems in the moment, hangs on the reply. Frank likes the idea of leaving it open, likes the idea that its tiny red pillow suggests a mouth on the verge of speech. But looking at it now, agape, the faux luxe fabric catching the light, he thinks it's vulgar. A dirty joke. "Closed," he says. Bean nods, his gravity probably ironic, but that's the only gear he's got.

The gang leaves the room, and Frank begins scouting out a place to hide (but not quite hide) the box somewhere. Nothing can be moved; it must be visible, not set behind books or under a bowl. Places high and low, cluttered and spare, present themselves to his appraising eye. He needs an inconspicuous spot but one—and here's the game's kick, at least for Frank tonight—so obvious that those who take a long time or simply can't find it will in the view of the others appear unperceiving, utterly lacking in reasoning powers. The box is square, matte gray and could easily blend with the brace of pale book spines on an upper shelf; it would also sit unobtrusively among an empty set of blockish stone candle holders; and it's hard to imagine anyone could spy it out if placed atop the cable modem. Of course, Jess would—her house, her lamp. But then, do we really know the things we live with? Frank was surprised just last week when he discovered the nightstand he bought years ago at a flea market and has slept right next to since then was inlaid around the drawer with interlocking swastikas. Albeit, the ancient Indian sort, but still, how had he missed that?

The players return and begin their search. Protocol dictates that when one person spots the item that person quietly takes their seat in such a way as to not reveal the hiding place. This continues until everyone's seated. When people begin sitting down, those still in the hunt panic; they are left out of the secret and their poking about takes on an increasingly comic cast. Barely suppressed sniggering can be heard as someone peers behind a vase or surveys a knickknack display while completely overlooking what's right in front of them. The freshly minted in-crowd sits back and enjoys the show—watching their friends flunk the test. But no one is sitting now, and they have all been sniffing around the in-between places for ten minutes.

With a sober mien yet giddy heart, Frank occupies himself folding and refolding the cuffs on his pants; he has to do something physical, something distracting, to refrain from exposing the depth of his delight. If it were somehow known, his thoughts broadcast to the room, *he* would become the object of derision. He likes the current balance of power—thus the leader once again takes careful stock of that cuff. *Never gonna find it.*

"I bet he stuck it up his ass," Bean says.

"Or up yours," Jack says. "You wouldn't notice."

"Christ, will you please," Sandy says. She's on tiptoe giving the window sashes the once over. "That hurts just hearing it go in."

Typical Sandy offering—weird, disturbing, and true if you really think about it.

They aren't going to find the ring box, or it's pretty doubtful. Although it would be simple enough and they certainly had the opportunity. Frank played another game growing up—the kids in his neighborhood were apprentice felons who would mature into bar fighters, meth peddlers, and wife beaters. Their sport was called Hide the Strap. It was just like this game only instead of a ring box or some other silly shit, you hid a belt and the person who found it could use it to lay on blows to everyone until they got back to base. Frank was often slow or sometimes tripped; who knows why, but he came home more than few times with long welts on his legs and short ones like bracelets on his arms. Once, though, he lagged behind, the last of the pack to round the corner into the empty lot where the belt would usually be hidden downfield in a coffee can or discarded tire. As he turned the corner, vigilant with trepidation, he saw it right there—the buckle poking out from the drain pipe of the garage at the edge of the lot. He drew it out and hid it in his jacket and then ambled into the lot with the others saying things like, "I hope I find it this time." At the far end of the lot, he positioned himself between Billy Henderson and the base. This asshole had recently singed him with particular glee. "Don't know where the thing is," he sighed, pulling it out and quickly doubling the strap for more control. "It's gotta be somewhere. . . ."

And, fact is, everything is somewhere and the ring box is right on the floor by the entry to the living room. Right on the floor. They all stepped right past it and no one has thought to turn around, to go back to the beginning. Frank enjoys their increasing agitation, although Jess has given up; she's staring out the window at a TV playing across the street. Still, he savors the triumph. It won't be as sweet as it was with Billy (which was only so sweet—a week later the prick sucker punched him in the school lavatory and knocked a front tooth loose). No, it won't be as good as it was that day in the lot, the strap whistling with every stroke. But it will be close.

Hot Hand

This strenuous and somewhat painful game is popular with boys and budding sociopaths of college age up to their first substance abuse rehabilitation. The game tests a young man's capacity to deliver as well as withstand pain; it also explores his erotic inclinations insofar as he may or may not enjoy the giving and receiving of said pain. Fraternity hazing, military boot camp, Stanley Milgram, and centuries of war crimes and inquisitions all come to mind. And for this reason, the players might consider being sworn to secrecy as revelations about participation in the game might one day impact a former player's defense strategy in a legal proceeding. First and foremost, though, we keep in mind that Hot Hand is all in good fun. And that belief when expressed through the clenched teeth of either the player dishing it out or taking it provides, it is reported, remarkable comfort.

The details: One man bends forward hands on knees, eyes blindfolded, or, better, he leans on a table with his head on his arms. A gym horse, if handy, conjures the appropriate locker room ambiance. Or better yet, over a carpenter's bench, which evokes an atmosphere of workmanlike competence. The other young men gather around, and after what the manual dubs "appropriate preliminaries," one of them gives a very vigorous swat with the palm of the hand to the man's backside. It behooves us to pause at that phrase and interrogate. It no doubt refers to the various stratagems—moving about, altering voices, creating distractions—the manual suggests in order to mask the identity of the swatter from the swattee, for that is the game's crux: the blindfolded player must attempt to name the man who hit him. But what other possible solicitations, excitations, and depredations might be classified under "appropriate preliminaries"? Does the blindfolded player teasingly invite his fellows to exercise maximum strength; does he instead beg for restraint, or simply to be released from the game itself? Are members of the group titillated by the imminent violence? Do they exhort one another to greater heights of anticipation and action? And finally, are there proceedings by which the power relation between the gathered men and the one man—bent over, sightless, and exposed—is given form? A ritual, perhaps. One involving the wearing of fedoras and invocations of Old Testament lore; or incense, feathers, and copious amounts of bear grease; or music—the chanted thrum of *Carmina Burana*?

With or without ceremony, a player approaches the buttocks, raised and available for common scrutiny. No implement is permitted—not a belt, switch, or lickin' stick. Nor poker, broom, or bamboo cane. The hand and hand alone delivers the blow: it is well fitted to the task, concave where the buttocks are convex, cushioned, but not too much so, and prehensile so as to take hold, if necessary, and finish the strike with a commanding grip. Only the hand furnishes the resounding clap that in the minds of the players is satisfyingly joined to the yelp that follows; that sound can be made even zestier if bare flesh is made available. Of course, this stylistic variation is typically a matter subject to a group vote, Robert's Rules pertaining to such. If permitted, the game's "hand" is indeed hot.

After the blow its object rises, faces his comrades, and tries to identify the man who has hit him. Those who possess an alert tactile sense are advantaged at this juncture—they consult their vivid impression of the striking hand's finger-girth and overall splay to match with what they now see. (For this and other less savory reasons, rules require the men to keep their hands out of their pockets.) Those gifted with other keen senses might use their recollection of, say, the hitter's breath which most likely came in a sudden burst due to exertion; that effort no doubt produced a groan that can also disclose the hitter if his voice is recognized. Often, though, among the young men who play this game frequently together, a general awareness develops about the kind of blow—its speed, placement, and finger-work—each player is prone to deliver. Each man's swat has its own signature. This accrued knowledge can lessen the competitive element, even as it amplifies group camaraderie.

If the guess is correct, the two trade places; if not, the same man is down again. (For some players, the repetition is borne as something of a lark; for others, it is a dire sentence. This is why the down man should get at least two guesses.) The guess can sometimes take on the tone of a plea or an accusation; it can be heard as a barely comprehensible cry of anger and disgust. Or it is made and acknowledged as if part of the sort of happy dispute—over sports teams or the difference between slant rhyme and assonance—men often engage in.

The jibes and banter will cease as the new down man dons the blindfold and bends into the proper position, and there is an opportunity for mindful reflection among those gathered. It is a time when they can consider their fellowship as well as the fleeting nature of those bonds, if not of youth itself. This hiatus in the merriment may be brief, but it should also be instructive: they will not always be as they are—strong, affably joined, and free to beat upon another man's ass with lighthearted abandon. These are the hours that in recollection will kindle warmth in aged hearts one day.

Vocal Blind Man's Bluff

Music, loud, insistent, and dissonant makes remaining calm difficult. Clanging bells, penny whistles, and what is probably a toy piano ride treble-high over a honking bass saxophone playing "Yakety Sax" at half-speed. It's a funeral march for a suicidal clown, or that's what Sandy surmises. She observes Bean at the kitchen table fiddling with his laptop, jumping from one noisy video to another and judges the probable success of hitting him from across the hall with the mug she squeezes with increased annoyance. Just thump him in the back. Divert his attention from playing whatever he's playing. As this only slightly violent thought discharges its modest current, she's conscious of the weight and hardness of the mug. An empathy too finely tuned allows her to absorb the sensation of being hit with it and there, in the big armchair, she flinches.

"Bean, please," Sandy says. To herself, though. Louder then, "Bean, please turn it down."

"Yeah, turn that shit off," Jack shouts as he descends the stairs. He holds his hands out, palms up. "Who took the towel out of the bathroom?"

"We need it for Blind Man's," Bean declares as he brandishes the purloined hand towel and calls the group to form a circle. People from Jack's office are here; some college friends of Jess's, too. No matter the increased numbers, he chooses Sandy—she knew he would as if in retribution for those angry thoughts—and soon her face from forehead to the tip of her nose is draped in a towel held in place with a binder clip that catches a hunk of her hair.

"Hey," she says. The towel smells like sink.

She sits in the big chair while they dance around her—yes, dance; it's not a pretty sight—until she gives a signal. She could clap, or shout "Stop." When everyone halts Sandy will point to one of the players and that person will have to make a vocal sound that's been determined in advance. They may have to imitate the sound of an animal named by the blind man, sing a song, speak in tongues, or impersonate Lucille Ball discovering a bat in her bedroom. Tonight, Sandy asked that those she selects cry like an eight-year-old who has been sent to their room for backtalk. She has one shot at identifying the player; if she succeeds, the two trade places. If she fails, she will continue drawing breath through what increasingly stinks of drainpipe.

The circular cavorting begins; the floor's vibrations make their way through the chair to Sandy. It's a pleasant sensation, like she's in a drink being stirred. She can't see anyone and they can't quite see her but she is at the center of things. She tightens a bit and calls out "Stop," and the vibration recedes. People laugh. Someone trips, it seems, into someone else and there's more laughing. Sandy stands, slowly turns, and with a regal flourish points into the darkness. She's pointing out there, out past the circle, to the living room. Out there.

It's a friend of Jess's, the woman with chipped fingernail polish who has been popping out all evening to smoke on the stoop. She begins with tiny moans, more sexual than sad, but then pushes them higher, allowing a raggedness to creep in around their edges. It's throaty and wet and everyone is quiet. They build quickly. Soon there's something undeniably genuine; the choking catch begins to spark some small alarm. She is wailing and heads turn away or down because there is fear that this woman's face will be streaked with tears. And then, as if a needle jumped its groove, the sound ceases and is replaced by her panting— healthy, exerciser's panting—as if she'd done a steep stretch on the elliptical trainer. Slack faced, smiling, she covers her mouth to cough. The room temperature drops a few degrees as the flush of embarrassment ebbs.

Sandy knows that crying; she hears all of its parts and pieces. In the dark, she can see it. Jagged streaks of chalk across a blackboard crisscrossing and swirling over and over until the blackness is almost hidden behind a veil of white dust and grit. And when it stops, she knows *who* is crying, too—the cough is the clue. She thinks about the fingernail polish, chewed away or just neglected. You would have to disown that cry wouldn't you? Sandy is about to say her name but doesn't. There's someone else here who could cry like that. There's someone whose name she says out loud with a little glee, with a little accusation.

Where Am I?

There are three things to think about that are almost always good things to think about, according to Sandy. It's good to think about her bedroom when she was eleven and her family lived in a stone farmhouse, the only such place among several suburban developments. They lived there for one year after moving while her family looked for a real house, one with air conditioning and windows that fully closed. Her bedroom was in the oldest part of the structure; with its low ceiling and deep window casements (where she loved to sit that winter because half of her would be warm and the window side would be cold) it was like a tower room in a castle. She can conjure every detail, from the dark lake of a stain on the wall by her bed to her purple plastic disc player perched on a high shelf so the music could wash down over her. It is also good to think about France; she visited an aunt there for two weeks during a summer in college. The woman had retired early to live in Aix but was suffering from a terrible depression when Sandy arrived. For nearly the entire two weeks the two talked all day in her small garden and went to bed early. Neither left the house much at all, but Sandy can easily fill an hour recalling the time there, the caterpillars in the overgrown garden, an afternoon at the open-air market in town, and the visit to Cezanne's studio, where they could only stay twenty minutes because they were mistaken about the closing time. All of France fits inside that garden and their conversations about how a strong morning dream could live with you all day or how when some people talk really fast you hear what they say as a kind of singing. And it is good to think about Jess. It is always good to think about Jess.

But Jess is a person not a place and Sandy is supposed to imagine that she is in some specific place, doing some definite thing. The others will ask her questions in an attempt to learn where she is and what she's doing. She will guide them with answers restricted to *yes* and *no*. Wide latitude is allowed: she's in the Library of Congress playing air hockey; inside Carlsbad Cavern performing sexual reassignment surgery; at the corner of Hollywood and Vine reciting the poems of Sappho; in a Sicilian convent sniffing glue. The first member of the team to guess the correct answer will be the imaginer. If no one guesses within a specified time the imaginer wins. Although locale and the activity performed there are limited only by one's inventive capacity, some players tend to return to particular themes. Bean is often somewhere exposed and sports related (the Rose Bowl, the Roman Coliseum, Mount Everest) where he is relieving himself. This more or less unvarying picture is Technicolor vivid in everyone's mind. The others manage a tad more variation—except Frank, who reliably does something heroic, like saving a toddler from alligators in the Everglades. If you guess his place, then all you have to do is figure out what disaster happens there.

If someone guesses within five minutes Sandy relinquishes her spot. But she's survived two rounds (in Dubuque ironing clothes; in the Coney Island Aquarium clipping her nails) by aiming for simplicity, stuff she's actually done—she believes the more elaborate the concoction the more affirmatives it yields. She would prefer to keep them guessing, as tonight she particularly enjoys watching disappointment on Jess's face tighten into irritation. She sees it even if no one else does. So she draws on a simple thing, a good thing because good things are just that: In the farmer's market in Aix buying fruit.

Bean starts, "Are you masturbating?" The only person who has ever answered yes is Bean himself. He doesn't care about guessing the place.

"No," Sandy says.

"Are you in the United States?" Jess asks.

"No."

"Are you in Europe?" Frank asks.

"Yes."

Frank goes again, "Are you in England?"

"No." There's a lot of this until they get to France, to Provence, to Aix. But the questions poke and prod everywhere but the commonplace. In the town square doing the tango; riding a horse through a fountain; fencing; naked jumping jacks (Bean); hunting truffles; smoking hash; swinging a scythe in the cathedral. Jack's smartphone is about to chime finito when Jess airily inquires, "Are you buying something?"

"Yes," Sandy pauses to let a second or two tick by.

"Food?"

"Yes."

"Outside, at the market near Place de l'Hôtel de Ville?" Jess has been to Aix, bought plums in that market. For a shoot once she painted some sad looking plums to look like the picture she took of the ones there. Cezanne plums. Sandy stalls even as Jess coaxes her by nodding *yes, yes*. She wanted one more round, a bit more time playing the person who knows something that other people don't.

"Yes, that's it!" Her voice rising to the top of the exclamation point. *So great you guessed it, Jess. We're like-minded. We're both thinking good things.*

Where are you? What are you doing? Those are the questions we ask one another all the time. We need to know the place on the map and the investigation, celebration, or chore that occupies you. Sandy declares she'll sit out the next round and this spurs some *boos*. As she slides past Jess she conducts the familiar micro-debate—give Jess's forearm a quick squeeze or not. Friends would do that, wouldn't they? One would say something about Aix, about the plums there. The other would say something easily and it would sound that way. The debate goes the way it goes with Sandy—*just leave it be*. The two women start to move past one another, each tensing, a careful two-step like the one commuters do moving around in the subway car. But when Sandy's almost free of the moment, a touch is felt. Reaching back,

Jess has drawn her hand across Sandy's lower back. It's nothing, really. Not a caress, to be sure. The kind of thing that happens all the time. The kind of thing that might just be a good thing.

Catch-the-Cane

The woman at the center of a circle formed by the people she knew for a brief time and now are at best minor figures in anecdotes that she doesn't even tell anymore holds a wand or similar stick; it is held upright on the floor by her finger on the upper end. Jess stands confidently despite a felt fragility; she's inwardly braced against a possible knock-down wind. Her long white shirt hangs down almost to the cuffs of her shorts; she is particularly aware of the bareness of her legs, the imposition of her sandals' straps between her toes. She is a tuning fork, alert to the air, to passing clouds, to everyone's attentive gaze. When she deems it just right, she removes her finger and calls a number taken by one of those who've gathered around her. (The surrounding bunch drew numbered tickets from a cookie jar when they descended from the dirigible where Jess keeps obscure memories.) Hearing the number penciled on the slip he clutches as if it were a dry cleaner's ticket for a jacket borrowed from a violent friend then soiled with chocolate sauce, one half-forgotten acquaintance dashes out and attempts to catch the stick (but really, in these rather fantastical circumstances, why not just go with a wand) before it falls to the ground.

In bygone days, when canes and the boater-wearing gents who tapped them along the sidewalk were more common, the game was called Catch-the-Cane. Or perhaps they were only common in MGM musicals and those movies, having so colonized our sense of history, encourage us to believe that canes were once employed as sartorial grace notes rather than mere ambulatory aids. In fact, canes may only have been employed by the elderly and infirm and the expression "catch the cane" may have been a euphemism for such a person's collapse and demise. *Who caught that cane?* some antique soul may have asked, wondering who inherited some old man's fortune.

Jess contemplates all this during the slowly evolving trice of the wand's fall. She often mulls over the subject of history, its construction and dissemination, the role of winners in its telling. The wand is falling, has fallen, and will fall again, she says, or would say, if a sweaty, meatball-shaped man weren't kicking up dust as he charges her. As a twister might bear down upon a shiny Airstream, this lumpy man, middle-aged, *Eraserhead* tee shirt, bears down on Jess. The tiniest hairs on her calves register the oncoming displacement of air. His scent arrives, too. Is he the guy down the hall in her first New York apartment who let her call the police when she was broken into? His apartment, the couch, even the phone smelled of burnt rubber . . . and patchouli. He is bent over, his arm trawling beneath him as an outstretched hand nears the still-plummeting wand.

Will he be the winner? Will he tell the story of this day, this round of this game? What history is taking shape as she shifts her weight to free one leg and kick that fucking wand hard? It lifts over the assembled heads and beyond the circle. The would-be-thief can't brake—he has given his all, without thought to consequence or whether or not he would crash into Jess, without thought at all to what such headlong pursuit might mean to that lovely white shirt, until now—and he trips trying to avoid her, his bulk splayed out in the dirt. Jess will retain proprietorship of the wand. Members of the circle will regroup and no doubt behold her anew. They will see her as a serious woman, one most conscious of the say that history will surely have about them all.

Uncle Joshua Died Last Night

The players sit in a circle, and the leader says to the one at her left, "My uncle Joshua died last night." The dire news lands with the impact of a thrown tissue. "That's too bad; how did he die?" asks the second player. Odd how the amplifying adverb *too* in fact diminishes our sense of the speaker's evaluation of just how bad a thing the uncle's demise is. Not one of the players understands this first clause to in any way express actual empathy. Aside from offering a shrug that acknowledges the generally mortal condition of all players everywhere, the clause serves as an emotional predicate to the more pertinent issue: how did this Joshua meet his end? Players want this information. How he died—whether he was eighty-eight and his heart failed as he slept or he was twenty-eight and was hollowed out by a parasite he picked up from hummus purchased at the local green market—bears on and may heighten each player's intimate awareness of his or her own death. The leader replies, "With one eye shut." As she delivers this detail, one revealing more about his mere appearance than the cause of death, she revels in the cryptic nature of her reply by closing one eye. She does so with placid ease, no squinting, as if she is merely pulling down a shade to shield her mental furnishings from direct sunlight rather than actually mimicking the death mask of her so recently departed relative. A cool customer.

Her inquisitor, the rules require, must close one eye, too. Perhaps not as suavely as she closed hers, but close it he must and keep it closed till the end of the game. The leader conducts the dialogue with everyone in the circle until everyone's eye is shut. In the wake of his victory over Bulgarian rebels, the Byzantine Emperor Basil II blinded ninety-nine of every one hundred men he captured leaving these one-eyed soldiers to lead their cohort home. This suggests historical precedent for strong faith in the abilities of the single-eyed: Basil must have valued depth perception as less than crucial to basic navigation. None of the players will be required to lead others on a long journey, but as they sit safely in comfortable chairs having voluntarily closed an eye, they nevertheless share a kinship with those maimed eleventh-century Bulgars. Like those unfortunates, the players' ambit is suddenly constrained; their world smaller. On the other hand, because there is less to see there is less to worry about.

The leader goes around again with the same declaration about Joshua and her friends field the same gestural sympathy and question the manner and mode of death. This time her reply is "With one eye shut and his mouth awry." Additional information, true, but again the precise cause is evaded, although the description of the mouth could indicate a stroke, with its attendant hypertonia of masticatory muscles. She suits the action by screwing her mouth to one side. Alternatively, this mien—sarcastic, dismissive—tells us that Joshua may have met his final judge with at least as much judgment, perhaps unimpressed by the distinguished thing itself or the whole post-death adjudication, deeming it yet another hoop to jump through like high school algebra, biopsies, or meeting a prospective mate's parents. Dead Joshua may have wished to live longer (again, was his exit expected or a surprise?) to avoid this ultimate accounting, or he may have apprehended, in the microsecond before consciousness went *poof*, nothing more than blankness, and it was this ceaseless void that caused his mouth to twist as if to say, "Great. Just fucking great." What the leader thinks about these possibilities is cloaked by her determination to ensure that each member of the circle remakes their face in her image—pirate-eyed and sour-mouthed; she walks from player to player offering directions and insisting that, once formed, their version of Joshua's last face remain frozen as if they were dead themselves.

Third round: "With one eye shut, his mouth awry, and one foot held high." Hanged men are said to ejaculate when the noose cracks their neck; mortally wounded soldiers cry out for their mothers; and the congested lungs of the aged sound their death rattle. What spasm in his lower extremities lifted Joshua's leg into the air, left his foot held high? Or is this a clue to the still obscured cause of death? A reasonable speculation has our uncle (players develop an increasingly significant degree of familiarity with the deceased) engaged in some decisive act of physical exertion: kicking a ball, kicking a dog, kicking and screaming, cheerleading, imitating the goose step while watching the History Channel, or attempting to plant his size ten right up your ass you dumb sunamabitch if you ever try to park here again. Any one of these scenarios could occasion mortal consequence—was a college football field or the driveway of his split-level the stage for Joshua's final act? The leader braces against the back of her chair—her face, owing to prolonged tensing, now appears clenched and angry—to raise a foot above her waist. Her leg quivers with the strain but no more than her voice as she orders the players to get their own legs up, to get that foot held high—in sad (or is it desperate?) commemoration of an uncle so recently with us.

For what will or will not be the last round, the leader announces "My uncle Joshua died last night." To her left, the player half whimpering, half snarling through his mashed-up mouth, asks the question that has bedeviled this evening, "That's too bad; how did he die?" "With one eye shut," she says, her voice also undone, at war with itself. "And his mouth awry. And one foot held high." The sweet scent of decay has entered the proceedings; it clings amid the closeness of the circled bodies. "And waving goodbye," she declares. Niece, mourner, leader, pantomimist of death, she steadies herself with one hand and sets the other to a metronomic wave. One by one, the answer settles its outcome on every player. Bye, bye, they all wave. Goodbye. They all keep the leader's time and sway in their seats. Uncle Joshua, dead. Cause unknown; his grimacing Cyclopean face testifies to what pains, what fates? As the players wave, genuine heartache begins to weigh on them, slowing their arms to motionless gesture—limp hands raised as if to say *Please stop*. The leader opens her closed eye. She unscrews her mouth, drops her foot to the floor and rises. Then she smooths her skirt slowly, her hands noticeably pressed against her hips and outer legs; the deliberateness suggests that of a faith healer whose ministrations seek to squeeze from a limb some deformity. "There's lemonade," she says. "For anyone who's thirsty."

Appropriate Cake

What cake would you bake for the devil?

Angel food cake.

What cake would you bake for a geologist?

Layer cake.

What cake would you bake for Aristotle?

A cake whose substance in the sense of existing in the form of a natural entity has the potential of life, that is to say it is moist.

What cake would you bake if an armed madman broke into your home and demanded that you produce a birthday treat or he will begin shooting, first the knees?

Lemon sprinkle cake. Or maybe a nice pecan coffee cake, light on the cinnamon, heavy on the Drano.

What cake would you bake for the devil?

Reconsidering. Isn't angel food cake just going to piss him off? Is that wise? Just give the prince of darkness what he wants—devil's food cake—and don't feel you have to fight the Son of God's battles for him.

What cake would you bake for the silent b?

Crumb cake.

What cake would you bake for a sculptor?

Marble cake is the obvious answer if your idea of sculpture is a century out of date. A computer screen wrapped in yarn perched on a packing crate cake is a tad more contemporary.

What cake would you bake for an idler?

Loaf cake. Or sponge cake if he's borrowing money from you while he forages for broken computers and packing crates to build his sculptures, a recent example of which he titled "Marble Cake" because you served that for dessert when he came for dinner for the umpteenth time this year and that is his way of saying thank you.

What cake would you bake for a gossip?

Spice cake.

What cake would you bake for a pirate or an accountant if he has an alcohol problem, is six years sober, and is currently in line for a promotion that you believe you deserve?

Rum cake.

What cake would you bake for a dogcatcher?

Pound cake. Outside of old cartoons does this occupation actually exist? Frankly, this list of cake recipients is growing improbable if not outright farcical. Or insulting. Say you do know a "dogcatcher," or animal rescue employee, in more acceptable parlance. Is this someone to whom you present, as a dinner guest in their home, with a broad and ingratiating smile, a pound cake?

What cake would you bake for someone you secretly despise owing to their insulting offer of a punningly dubbed dessert that reminded everyone at your party that your job involves putting animals to sleep?

Yellowcake.

Buried Words

Where do words that are thought but go unspoken go? Sandy ponders the question as this game commences. Do they lodge in the brain that forms them, or in the throat where they are first felt as inchoate sound, or do some, the strongest, falter and come to rest in the mouth of the would-be speaker? She could ask this question; she might. Then again, no. It would come out wrong. Silly. Pretentious. Where then does the unsaid settle? Jess distributes pencils and slips of paper. A proverb or a famous quote will be announced, and each player writes it on a sheet of paper, she explains. The fifteen-second clock starts as they write down as many hidden words as they can form by combining successive letters. "In the order they appear," Jess enunciates the directive with clipped precision. She holds up and reads from a sheet on which she's written *appearances are often deceitful* and underneath a list of buried words: *pear, ear, ran, an, ten, tend, end, deceit,* and *it.* "And no one-letter words. That's desperate." Jess is squinting. Sandy knows she dislikes wearing her glasses. She used to get away with that, but lately there's been the squinting. She's not quite conscious of doing it, Sandy's pretty sure. If she were, the squint wouldn't be so candid—her face bunched so tight you can almost taste the lemon she looks like she sucked on. She'll catch on soon, but until then the apparent absence of vanity is disarming—even if its cause is, well, vanity.

A familiar one, the first proverb for parsing: *A stitch in time saves nine*. Most everyone finds what's to be found, *itch*, *hint*, *mesa*, *chin*. Bean believes he's the only one who will write out *tit*, but everyone has it. Frank is the winner, successfully arguing that *ave* may be Latin but it counts—it's in somewhat common usage, at least for, as he puts it, fans of kitschy wedding renditions of "Ave Maria." "The correct pronunciation," he notes, "is ah-way."

"That's a fact," Bean says. "Same *w* for your name . . . Wank." This is so dumb everyone breaks up, even Wank.

"The sharpener, please," Jess says. When she writes she bears down on the page, her scribbled words look pressed into the loose leaf. Is she worried, Sandy wants to ask, that between the writing and the reading the letters will slip off the page if they aren't held fast? The fluorescent overhead in Sandy's kitchen buzzes in fits and starts. The light, too, varies in brightness. If you're bored and you begin paying attention to this, it's unnerving. That's Jack. It makes him think they're all subjects in a lab experiment. Maybe Frank agrees; he's growing ever more antsy, caught as his senses are between the light's perturbations and the refrigerator's on and off again motor. An electric hum is circling his head. It's like a fly, but one that can dart right through your skull.

Familiarity breeds contempt yields *liar*, *tempt*, *am*, *con*, and *reed*. No one is happy about excavating *snot* from *There's no time like the present*. Bean honestly doesn't know that *Absence makes the heart grow fonder* doesn't give you *sense*. When ridiculed about this he mumbles about alternative spellings in Middle English. It's Jess's turn and she opts for a quote; she saw it in a magazine at the gym yesterday in an article about Marilyn Monroe and feminism. The actress, Jess declares, said "Men are willing to respect anything that bores them."

Sandy perks up—she likes this one, likes that Jess came up with it, and contemplates her list. *Will, or, ore, any, ESP* (it's a noun, not just an acronym; she knows this from a crossword puzzle she did not long ago), *hem, hat, tan, ill*. With maybe two seconds before the cell phone dings, she sees *tore*. Not an easy one to find, the way it bridges the preposition and a word—*respect*—quite foreign, it seems to her, from a word that causes separation. Sudden, harsh separation. The past tense of tear. And that word, too, with its *tea* and its *ear*. This rumination runs its course in a flash, but that's still too long for her to write the whole word down. She barely scribbles *to* before the chime goes off. The words look lonely to her, disconnected to anything useful—like tiny pieces shaken out from the inside of something broken. Sandy's pause, paper in hand, is quietly acknowledged by her friends and their vocal restraint is palpable. What do they think I'm thinking? Sandy shakes her head as if to ward off any telepathic intrusion. Finally, Jess broaches a request: "Come on, show us what you've got." Sandy starts reading from her list. "Will," she says, mustering her matter-of-fact tone. But that won't change anything; she knows they'll still hear the word as the beginning of a question she's about to ask.

Dropping the Dime

The player lies flat on her back with a dime on her nose and tries to dislodge it by humming the Four Tops hit, "It's the Same Old Song." Memories of a love that used to be crowd Jess's thoughts. Ladies' choice in the gymnasium; brown bagging at the Dairy Queen. A tingling warms her face as images from the past flex within, but the coin does not move. The middle eight bars feature a saxophone solo and she must imitate this interlude by humming deeper, growing guttural, until the chorus resumes and she can return to her reverie. If the dime slips from her nose, she may not notice. A player who knows her well—who would that be in this room, on this night?—should pick it up and remark to the other players that such a small denomination was once worth something but now it's not. Instead, after a long time everyone leaves while Jess remains supine, uncertain about rising. Perhaps unable.

Compared to What?

While one player is out of the room, others choose some object in plain sight. The odd player enters and approaches the others in turn, saying to each one, "Compare it to me." The respondent must, by truth or fancy, indicate some similarity. Answers may be far-fetched but not pointless. Answers may be eloquent but not verbose. Answers may be hurtful but not assaultive. Some players will be clever; others not so. Distinctions based on upbringing, social class, and taste in home decor will take on unexpected prominence. Some players will believe they've been sucker punched. Others will revel in their assumed superiority. Bean may choose a letter opener because he sees Jess as smooth and hard as metal. Or Frank might choose an envelope because he believes she is closed to the world, yet awaiting an intrusion upon her privacy. Sandy retrieves a spoon from her bag to indicate that Jack is useful, connected to essential needs; Jess, too, compares Jack to a spoon—easily handled, accommodatingly curved. Jack will say Sandy is like a pillow on the couch because she can be moved to just the right spot; Frank thinks she's a coaster: protective, an intermediary, but one that you hardly know is there. Bean, everyone agrees, is the remote control. Players will likely deem such comparisons facile, carrying the damply introspective air of book club meetings. Eyes are rolled; certain assumptions about public schooling are confirmed. The room grows tense; all ironic disdain drains away from among the participants. They are left with, figuratively, the clothes they wear on laundry day: frayed, soiled, and inexcusably reeking of themselves.

Lame Fox and Chickens

The fox stands at the center of a circle, runners—let's cast their part in line with the cliché, we'll call them chickens—are scattered randomly about. The chickens tantalize the fox by entering the circle and taunting him with such expressions as "Lame fox, lame fox, you are but a mote of dust in the eye of God," or "Lame fox, lame fox, you reek of unrighteous anger," or "Lame fox, lame fox, shame on your lame-fox self." Impervious to their jibes, the fox pursues his tormentors, his cute fox nose twitching at the scent of meat. But he can only run within the circle. Once he steps outside this conjectural border the fox must—and this is no joke—hop. He's lame. Such a development risks the chickens confusing this game with others such as "Run, Rabbit, Run" and "Peg-Leg Shepherd and Wolf," but they're not quite the fools we might suppose as we observe from a distance sundry heads and legs in hectic array.

Fact is, their level of strategy is mercilessly acute. They have sacrificed what they might know about themselves to better know the game they play. They know the lame fox isn't really lame, but rather feigns disability in order to lull his potential victims into complacency; they know the lame fox wishes to free himself from the circle and could easily do so as the circle is a mere fabrication, but the fox also wants all concerned to believe in the circle, the fact of its enclosure, because such a circle predicates a center, a center at which the fox is pleased to find himself. Both fox and chickens, pursuer and pursued, know what one another knows; yet this doesn't mean equilibrium exists between the two. "Lame fox, lame fox, come out of your den," the players shout in unison. Schoolyard singsong creeps into their chant; they are the many, the fox, the few. Their inchoate will is an ever-expanding force that seeks material form. Gradually the circle, for the fox, comes to resemble a cone, steep and echo-mad, and he finds himself pacing at its bottom, the voices booming down upon him. Once the fox roamed widely, discreetly—a blur in night's smallest hours. The circle's promise of eminence was phantasmal. *How did this happen?* he asks himself. *How did these birds, their brains the size of buttons, steal my range, my solitude?*

Alphabetical Adverbs

One player selects an adverb, and the others try to guess it. Each player might reluctantly confess to his or her self-doubt. They might then attest to uncertainty's inelegance when introduced to lovemaking; its failure as a spur to accomplishment, as well as its strong correlation to the frequent use of household cleansers. When the adverb is guessed after what can often be two to three hours of labored interrogation, it is written down and eagerly entrusted to the most disliked person in the group. How this individual is determined depends in equal parts on regional custom and the players' variable dispositions to cruelty. One player raps the table hoping to summon spirits. Another one speaks about her encounters with frictional resistance. A third unbuckles his belt. These actions remain pure of any awareness of their origins in the players' biological reflexes. The friends will be said to score points excitedly, lose gracefully, and turn their faces into masks purposefully. But these actions do not require modification; they are only what they are. Because players do what the rules tell them to do—that's how you play the game. A door opens, an authoritative voice makes evident what everyone has known all along: the time to end one thing and begin another has unavoidably arrived.

Acknowledgments

The author would like to thank the MacDowell Colony for the residency during which much of this book was written and the Council of Literary Magazines and Presses for its award of a FACE OUT grant. Portions of this book appeared in the *Brooklyn Rail* and in a chapbook published by Belladonna.

About the Author

Albert Mobilio is the author of *Bendable Siege*, *The Geographics*, *Me with Animal Towering*, and *Touch Wood*. His poems and essays have appeared in *Harper's*, *Black Clock*, *BOMB*, *Cabinet*, *Hambone*, *Jacket*, *Open City*, and *Tin House*. A recipient of a Whiting Award, an Andy Warhol Foundation Arts Writers Grant, and a MacDowell Fellowship, he is an assistant professor of literary studies at The New School's Eugene Lang College, a contributing editor at *Bookforum*, and an editor for *Hyperallergic Weekend*.